GRAVITIC ATTITUDE STABILIZER (P/S)

BRIDGE

Profile

NAVIGATION AND TARGET AQUISITION ARRAYS

BABYLON 5
SECURITY
MANUAL

PRIMARY DRIVERS (3)

Bottom

Top

PHOTIC PULSE WEAPONS (4)

0   50 meters

Front   Back

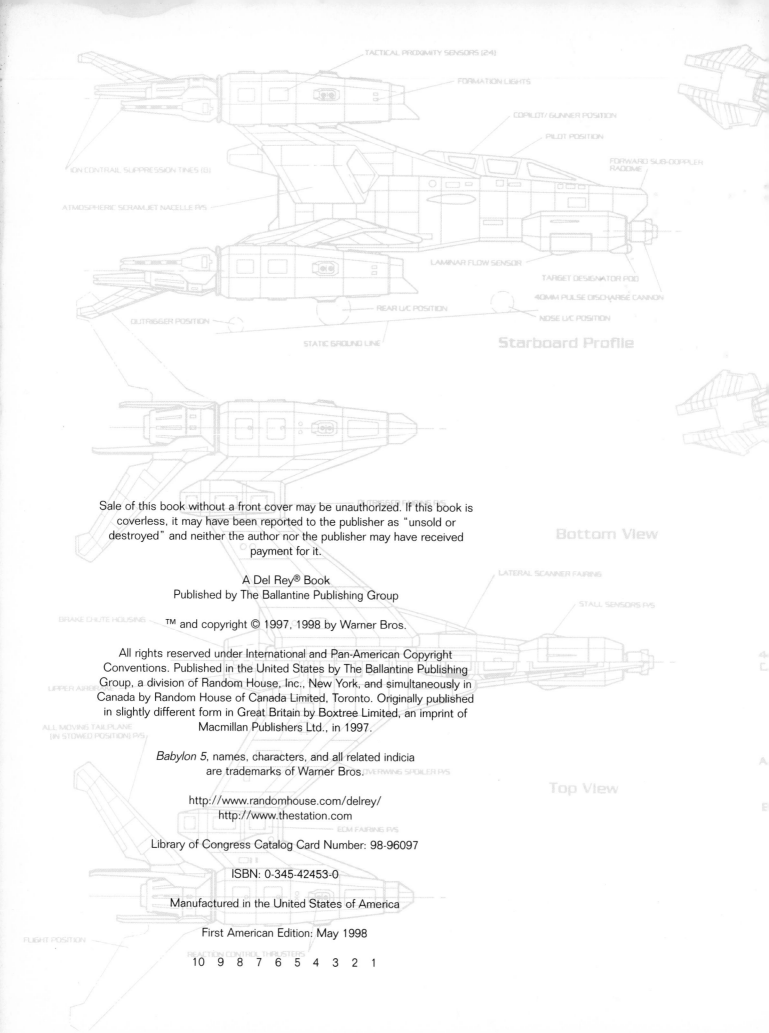

A Del Rey® Book
Published by The Ballantine Publishing Group

™ and copyright © 1997, 1998 by Warner Bros.

http://www.randomhouse.com/delrey/
http://www.thestation.com

Library of Congress Catalog Card Number: 98-96097

ISBN: 0-345-42453-0

Manufactured in the United States of America

First American Edition: May 1998

10 9 8 7 6 5 4 3 2 1

BABYLON 5
SECURITY
MANUAL

JIM MORTIMORE
WITH ALLAN ADAMS & ROGER CLARK

DEL REY

The Ballantine Publishing Group • New York

CONTENTS

The *Babylon 5 Security Manual* **was updated by the new Security Chief, Zack Allan, on January 1, 2262. However, it is based on earlier manuals by the previous Chief of Security, Michael Garibaldi**

Welcome to Babylon 5 by Chief Warrant Officer Michael Garibaldi

What Is Babylon 5?

Basically, what you've got here is a big tin can in outer space. It's five miles long, and it's full of people: 250,000 of them on average. They all think they know the rules better than you do. Your job is to show them they don't. But you can't just jam a PPG rifle in their nasal cilia and say, "Yo, bud, can't drop that bubblegum there." You've got to know how to treat them right. Or make them THINK you're treating them right, even when you ain't. This is called DI-PLO-MA-CY.

Count the syllables. If the law of averages is with me, some of you greenies can probably even pronounce it. But here's the rub: now you've got to practice it. You've got to know how these folks tick. There's more than forty alien species here. There's over 30,000 nationalities and religions. Which is more than last year's crowd for the Mutai finals. It's the people that make this place work.

Understanding the people will make your job easier, and if your job's easier, my job's easier. (But not too easy: that's the difference between a pay raise and being made redundant.) Any bribes you get, keep to yourself. Anything else you get, I don't wanna know about it. Anything ELSE you get, medlab is on Blue 1.

Who Lives and Works Here?

YOU do. The only way off is through the Big Dark, and unless you want to make that trip without a space suit and thruster pack, you've got to learn to get along with everyone else who lives and works here. Can you say DI-PLO-MA-CY? I'm not saying things are rough, but we're not exactly the Mars Hilton, if you know what I mean. We're a frontier city. We get the lowlifes, the scum, the drunks. In my time here we've had looters and racists, murderers, thieves and conmen, cardsharks, dice blunters, doppelgangers, hijackers, and hooch sellers. Mad bombers and soul suckers we get every second Wednesday. Every one of them thinks he's got a special permit to break the rules. So far I haven't seen one permit that isn't printed in invisible ink on paper that doesn't exist. And by the way, if anyone finds the perp responsible for printing these "permits," well, just you lock him up good and proper, and we can all have a nice long holiday. That's a joke, by the way; living here's not. Learn the difference. It could save your life.

The Chain of Command

There's them, there's you, there's me, and there's God. In that order. The Buddhist philosophy suggests their god has nine billion names and that if anyone knows them all, the universe will end. For the purposes of rank, our god has just one name, Captain John Sheridan, and if you forget it, your universe will definitely end. With a bang. That bang will be the passenger air lock of the very next transport home clanging shut behind you.

Witty Pep Talk

To quote Captain Sheridan: "Everything dies. You, me, fashion, religion, everything. Right? WRONG. I'll tell you what doesn't die: honesty, integrity, passion. The first casualty of war is truth, and I tell you, Michael, we're at war. We're the foot soldiers, the pike bearers, the sergeants, and the generals. But we're also the enemy. Confused? Good. Through confusion comes clarity; through clarity, truth; through truth, victory."

Anyone who has a problem with this metaphor can take it up with the captain at the weekly Security review, Wednesdays at 0630 sharp. Don't forget to load your guns. And spit out that gum.

MICHAEL GARIBALDI
Chief Warrant Officer, Babylon 5, 2260

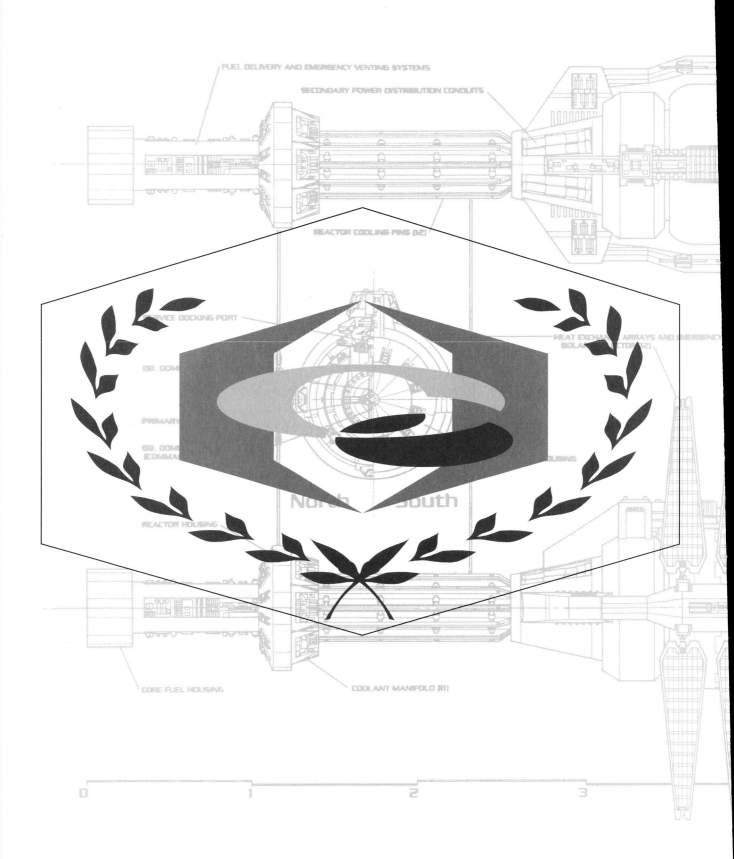

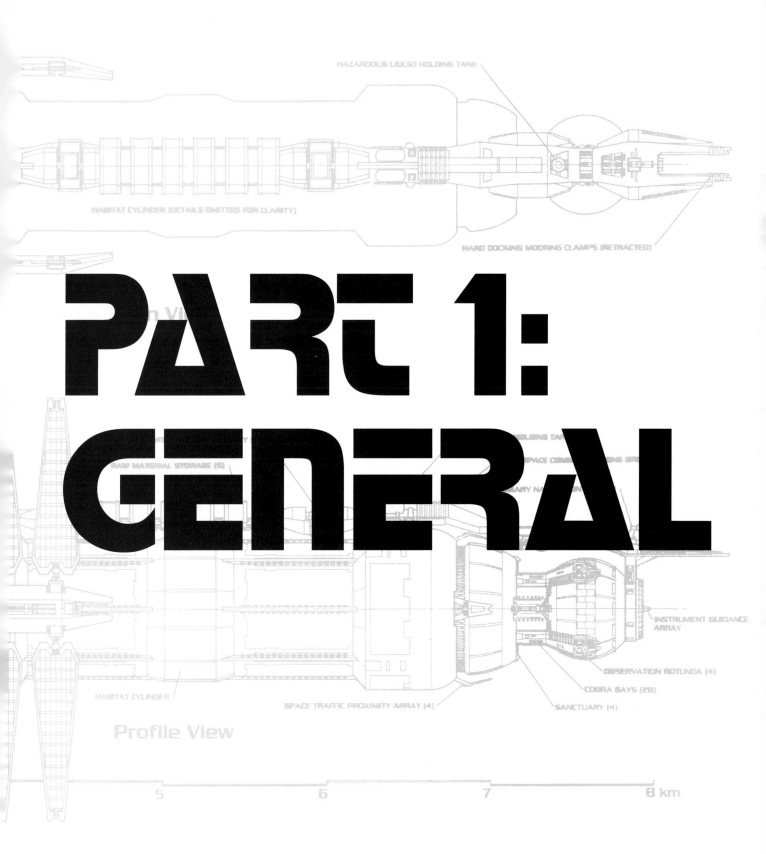

HAZARDOUS LIQUID HOLDING TANK

HABITAT CYLINDER (DETAILS OMITTED FOR CLARITY)

HARD DOCKING MOORING CLAMPS (RETRACTED)

PART 1:
GENERAL

INSTRUMENT GUIDANCE
ARRAY

OBSERVATION ROTUNDA (4)

COBRA BAYS (28)

HABITAT CYLINDER

SPACE TRAFFIC PROXIMITY ARRAY (4)

SANCTUARY (4)

Profile View

5   6   7   8 km

1.1 INTRODUCTION

Unit 1: Station Overview

What Is Babylon 5?

History prompts us to take into consideration the past whenever we view the future. Babylon 5 is an embodiment of this philosophy. Conceived and built by a multinational, multispecies consortium, Babylon 5 is situated at the point of juxtaposition of five major cultures and thirty-seven minor cultures (collectively referred to as the Non-Aligned Worlds). That makes Babylon 5 the hot seat in more ways than one.

What Is Babylon 5's History?

As its name implies, Babylon 5 is the fifth in a series of projects with similar design philosophies. Babylon Stations 1 through 3 were destroyed by acts of sabotage, using design flaw, accident, or terrorism. Babylon 4 disappeared without a trace on the day it became operational. Completion of Babylon 5 was secured through the financial intervention of the Minbari—and to a lesser extent other races. The command structure of Babylon 5 was linked directly to the EarthForce military. Now, due to their financial support and the station's secession from the Earth Alliance, the Minbari Grey Council has been granted considerable input into the policy-making process. The Minbari have chosen to exercise their right only once: in the selection of Babylon 5's first commanding officer, Commander Jeffrey Sinclair. Sinclair left Babylon 5 to serve as special envoy to the Minbari government. He was later declared missing in action after an incident involving Babylon 4's reemergence from a space-time anomaly.

Captain John Sheridan

Handpicked by Earth Alliance president William Morgan Clark to replace first-choice Babylon 5 CO Jeffrey Sinclair, Sheridan is career military, decorated three times, most prominently for his services at the Battle of the Line, in which he became the only EarthForce officer ever to bring about the destruction of a Minbari warship.

Commander Jeffrey Sinclair

Despite an exemplary career, Sinclair did not even appear on the short list drawn up by EarthGov for possible commanders of Babylon 5. Sinclair was promoted to officer in charge only at the insistence of the Minbari Grey Council, which never gave a reason for its choice.

**Earth Alliance Station
Babylon 5**

Location:	L5 point, Epsilon 3, Epsilon Eridani star system
Function:	Freight movement and political forum
Displacement:	2.5 million metric tons
Capacity (freight):	5–15,000 metric tons (dry) per twenty-four-hour period, 2–5,000 metric tons (wet) per twenty-four-hour period
Capacity (Species):	100,000 terrestrial, 150,000 nonterrestrial, 50,000 nonterrestrial/exotic

What Is Babylon 5's Purpose?

Babylon 5 is a self-sufficient frontier city. It is neutral ground, both a political forum and a galactic marketplace. This may appear to some as a contradiction; history shows us that to differentiate between the two concepts is folly. Therefore, the design philosophy of Babylon 5 (and the preceding stations) is to use the physical location and size of the station to create an environment where aliens and Humans may work together to further the cause of each group. It is "Human" nature to seek comfort in the future: together we will find it.

1.2 STATION LAYOUT

Geography

To assist travel in-station, all sectors are color coded. They consist of Yellow, Red, Blue, Grey, and Green, and then one of 36 sector numbers each denoting a 10-degree region, and then a level or deck number (Grey 17, 13). Areas with zero-g are designated Yellow.

There are various locator graphics throughout the station: three dots in a line above and through three larger circles for the Core Shuttle, a single dot over a bar for living quarters, six dots to either side of a bar for a meeting room, etc.

Internal directions are denoted by spinward, retrograde, forward (toward the command sphere), and aft (toward the recyclers).

Personnel

Most Humans on the station are civilian contractors, such as those handling dock work and food preparation, under contract to Babylon 5. Others, such as the technicians in the Observation Dome, medical staff, command staff, and Security, are now privately contracted by and work for Babylon 5. In total there are 1,500 guild dock workers and 6,500 other station personnel.

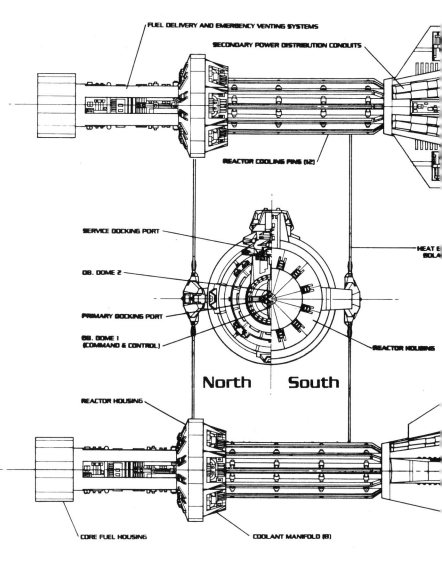

FUEL DELIVERY AND EMERGENCY VENTING SYSTEMS

SECONDARY POWER DISTRIBUTION CONDUITS

REACTOR COOLING FINS (12)

SERVICE DOCKING PORT

OB. DOME 2

HEAT E
SOLA

PRIMARY DOCKING PORT

OB. DOME 1
(COMMAND & CONTROL)

REACTOR HOUSING

North   South

REACTOR HOUSING

CORE FUEL HOUSING

COOLANT MANIFOLD (8)

0   1   2   3

General

(All dimensions are in multiples of station length.)

The station's total length is five miles, and the diameter of the largest rotating section is 0.094x.

The Yellow Sector cargo stabilizer is approximately 0.094x long, although it extends only 0.075x out from the main body of the station. Blue Sector is 0.187x. Grey Sector is 0.019x long. Red Sector is 0.047x long. Brown Sector is 0.085x. Green Sector is 0.075x. The main carousel is 0.547x long. The radiator vanes are 0.103x, and the fusion reactors are 0.35x long.

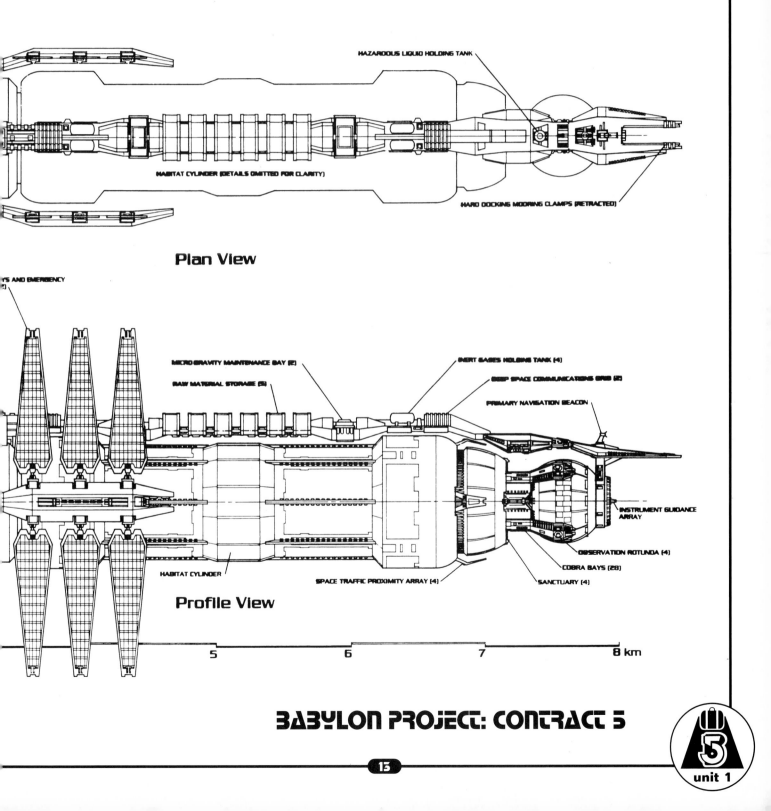

HAZARDOUS LIQUID HOLDING TANK

HABITAT CYLINDER (DETAILS OMITTED FOR CLARITY)

HARD DOCKING MOORING CLAMPS (RETRACTED)

Plan View

YS AND EMERGENCY

MICRO GRAVITY MAINTENANCE BAY (2)

RAW MATERIAL STORAGE (5)

INERT GASES HOLDING TANK (4)

DEEP SPACE COMMUNICATIONS GRID (2)

PRIMARY NAVIGATION BEACON

INSTRUMENT GUIDANCE ARRAY

OBSERVATION ROTUNDA (4)

COBRA BAYS (28)

SANCTUARY (4)

HABITAT CYLINDER

SPACE TRAFFIC PROXIMITY ARRAY (4)

Profile View

5   6   7   8 km

BABYLON PROJECT: CONTRACT 5

unit 1

Yellow Sector

Located aft of the Grey Sector and the carousel, Yellow Sector does not rotate. It contains the variable-g research labs as well as the primary fusion core and the associated subsystems. Cooling fins run the length of the sector, located on the outside of the hull.

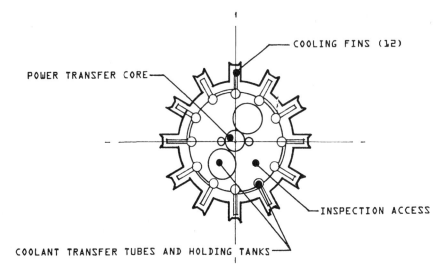

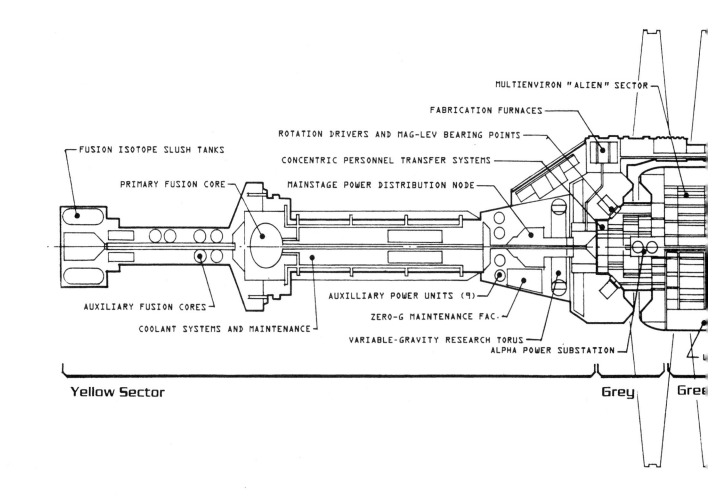

Yellow Sector

Grey   Gree

LOW-G DOCKING BAYS (4)

FUEL STORES

TRAVEL TUBES

Cargo bay

DOCK WORKERS' QUARTERS

DOCKING BAYS (24)

MAINTENANCE FACILITIES

Spaceship docking

Blue Sector

Blue Sector consists of seventy decks. It houses the maintenance and operations control centers, the normal and low-g docking bays, customs and embarkation, the dock workers' quarters, and the public Observation Dome. C&C also can be found in this sector. Access to Blue Sector is restricted to command personnel, except in medical emergencies.

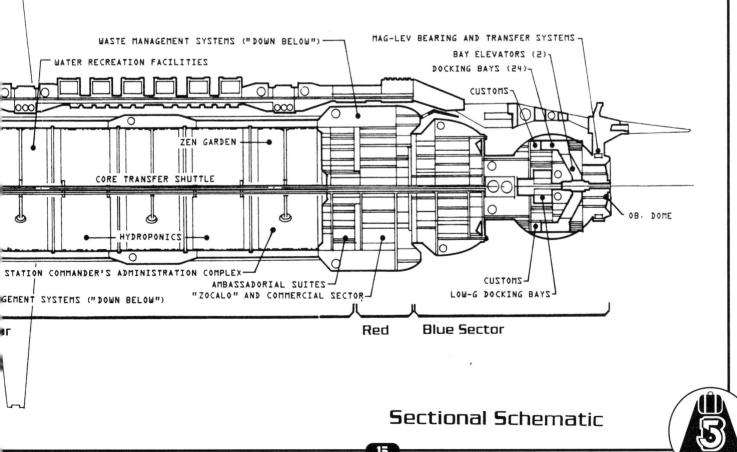

WASTE MANAGEMENT SYSTEMS ("DOWN BELOW")

MAG-LEV BEARING AND TRANSFER SYSTEMS

BAY ELEVATORS (2)

DOCKING BAYS (24)

WATER RECREATION FACILITIES

CUSTOMS

ZEN GARDEN

CORE TRANSFER SHUTTLE

OB. DOME

HYDROPONICS

STATION COMMANDER'S ADMINISTRATION COMPLEX

AMBASSADORIAL SUITES

CUSTOMS

"ZOCALO" AND COMMERCIAL SECTOR

LOW-G DOCKING BAYS

GEMENT SYSTEMS ("DOWN BELOW")

Red   **Blue Sector**

Sectional Schematic

unit 1

Red Sector

Red Sector is the main marketplace and business area. Together with service facilities such as Medlab 1, the Judiciary, Security Central, and the holding cells, the principal areas of note here include the Zocalo, hotel suites, casinos, bars, legal brothels, and stores of all types. Red Sector is a public area. Civilian access is granted at all times.

Diplomatic immunity

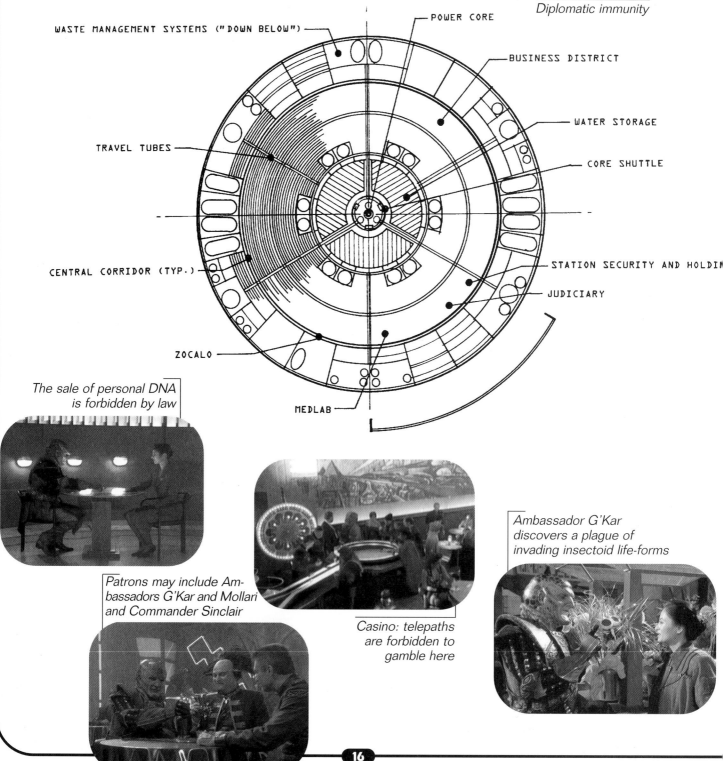

WASTE MANAGEMENT SYSTEMS ("DOWN BELOW")

POWER CORE

BUSINESS DISTRICT

WATER STORAGE

TRAVEL TUBES

CORE SHUTTLE

CENTRAL CORRIDOR (TYP.)

STATION SECURITY AND HOLDIN

JUDICIARY

ZOCALO

MEDLAB

The sale of personal DNA is forbidden by law

Patrons may include Ambassadors G'Kar and Mollari and Commander Sinclair

Casino: telepaths are forbidden to gamble here

Ambassador G'Kar discovers a plague of invading insectoid life-forms

Alien inhabitant of Grey 17

Grey Sector

The Grey Sector is adjacent to the aft end of the carousel. The fabrication furnaces, rotation drives for the principal mag-lev bearings, and the alpha power station are located here. The atmosphere monitoring station and maintenance facilities are next to the hull. The structure is incomplete due to financial restrictions. Scans are frequently ineffective in this sector, and communication levels on either side of deck 17 are unreliable at best. Deck 17 itself cannot be accessed due to computer/elevator malfunction and is currently under

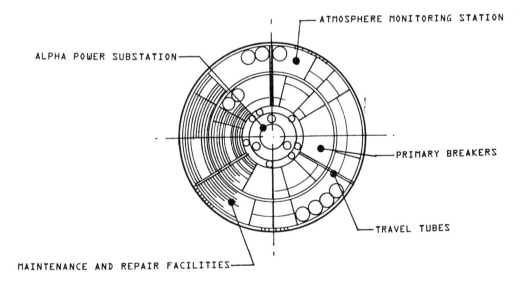

investigation. Rumors of missing personnel and religious cults are linked with Grey Sector; hence, access is restricted to maintenance, Security, and command personnel, except in medical emergencies. Deck 17 is off limits to all but Security personnel.

Green Sector

Green Sector is adjacent to the forward end of the Zen Garden and contains ambassadorial suites and associated chambers. Green Sector has multiple BabCom access points and is one of the main areas of focus for the Security Department. In recent years there has been an increase in diplomatic missions, and more governments are establishing embassies on the station. As space on Babylon 5 is tight, it is not possible to give everyone offices. Communal offices, meeting rooms, and conference rooms are available, as is access to the station's business facilities. Access is restricted to ambassadors and their staff and to command and Security personnel. Civilian access is denied except by permission of ambassadors or command staff.

Diplomatic relations require special training

Narn quarters

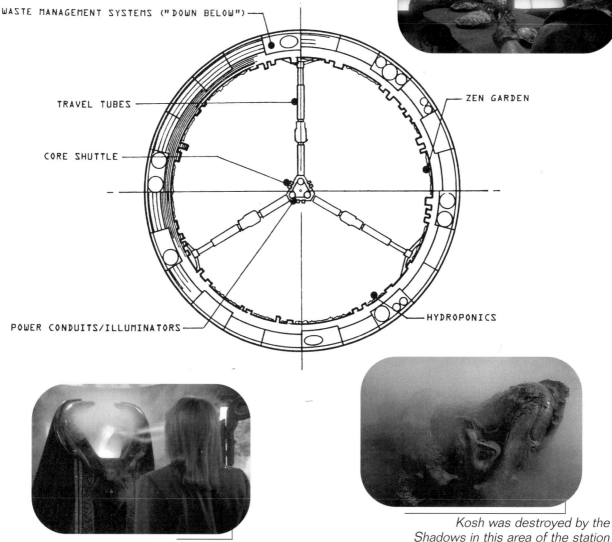

WASTE MANAGEMENT SYSTEMS ("DOWN BELOW")

TRAVEL TUBES

CORE SHUTTLE

ZEN GARDEN

POWER CONDUITS/ILLUMINATORS

HYDROPONICS

*Vorlon symbiosis
as staged in Green Sector*

*Kosh was destroyed by the
Shadows in this area of the station*

**Green
Sector
Activity**

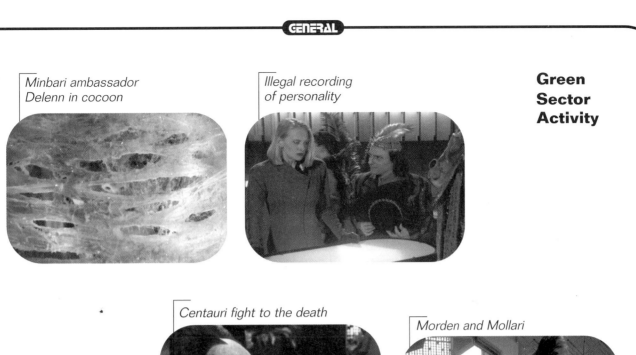

Minbari ambassador
Delenn in cocoon

Illegal recording
of personality

Centauri fight to the death

Morden and Mollari

Earth Alliance attempts
to bribe Sheridan

Vir Cotto and the
Centauri ambassador

Sheridan's wife,
Anna

Garibaldi with his motorbike

unit 1

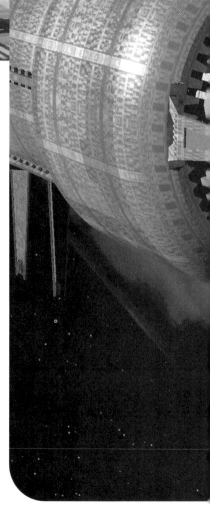

Shuttle bay

Docking Bays

The docking bays are located within the command sphere and the zero-gravity spine. There are sixty bays. Ships enter through the axis of the sphere after first matching station rotation. Large or zero-g dependent cargos are off-loaded in Yellow Sector. Certain bays are reserved for ambassadorial ships. (Bay 13 housed the Vorlon ambassador.) Access is restricted to guild members and station personnel. Civilian access is denied except when provision is made for crews of off-loading transports.

Delenn's diplomatic shuttle

GROPOS debarking transports on B5

Lumati cruiser approaches Babylon 5

Docking bay activity: Dr. Everett Jacobs being shielded from biomedical scanners by Vorlons

5

unit 1

Docking Bays—Potential Clients

Any sentient being with a spaceship is entitled to use this space, subject to docking fees and proof of nonbelligerence.

Seven Tango Seven

Narn cargo ship Tal'Quith *crashing in the docking bay*

ASIMOV

The Asimov *passenger liner*

HYPERION
An Earth Alliance ship

HYPERION

EARTHFORCE 1

Narn fighter

Earth Alliance
atmospheric shuttle

*Damaged
Soul Hunter ship*

unit 1

Cobra Bays

Located immediately behind the command sphere, the Cobra Bays provide exit only for EarthForce Starfuries. Reentry is via the main axis port. Alpha, Delta, and Zeta wings have up to 15 Starfuries each. Access is restricted to military, command, and Security personnel. Civilian access is STRICTLY DENIED.

COBRA BAYS

Living Areas

The living areas have to accommodate different environments and atmospheres. Some alien sectors are uninhabitable to Humans without protective breathing gear or other measures. Heavy CO_2 breathers and methane breathers have to wear appropriate respirators or encounter suits to travel among the Humans on the station. It is worth noting here, to avoid confusion, that the Human sections of the station are referred to as the alien sector by non-Human occupants. Life support can handle approximately 250,000 entities (some of which are described as a "transient population"; i.e., they are visiting the station).

There are two main means of transportation within the station: the transport tubes and the Core Shuttle. The Core Shuttle travels along the axis in low-g, while the transport tubes are similar to elevators and move from level to level.

The station operates on Earth Mean Time (EMT) whenever possible. Alien sectors may use alternative night/day cycles.

Exterior: Spine and Zero-g Sections

Running for the entire length of the rotating carousel section, the spine provides laboratory space for zero-g commercial research as well as the twin cargo stabilizers that provide a guide for transports delivering zero-g dependent cargos. Located north of the carousel are the fusion reactors, which extend over a fifth of the overall length of the station. Heat exchangers, solar fins, and waste reclamation units are also located here. Access is restricted to guild workers and Security personnel.

Maintenance 'bot's view of exterior hull

Heat dissipation units

Babylon 5 forward profile

THE CORE SHUTTLE
Please remove all personal belongings when exiting the Core Shuttle

Core

The public transport Core Shuttle System is located along the axis of the carousel and runs the entire length of the station. Civilian access is restricted only in designated emergency situations such as hull breach, terrorism, and fire.

Fusion Reactor

The fusion reactor section extends over a third of the length of the station. There are eight Tokamac 790 high-energy general fusion reactors with an approximate output of 73 Googolwatts. The waste from the reactors is stored in a hazardous materials storage site situated in a following orbit 7 km away from the station. Access is restricted to guild workers and Security personnel except in designated emergencies.

FUSION REACTOR

Central Corridor

This is the main public area. The Security detail here includes normal policing duties and maintaining order.

ZOCALO

unit 1

Biosphere of Babylon 5

The Garden

The Garden is a large botanical area that runs along the inside surface of the carousel. Rotation provides near–Earth Normal gravity at "ground level." Access is by public Core Shuttle. Window/mirror systems allow sunlight from the Epsilon star to enter in on an artificially maintained night and day cycle. At ground level, the Garden contains farmland, limited woodland, a hedge maze, a mosque, a Zen Garden, artificial lakes, hydroponic gardens, and areas for waste reclamation. Below ground level is twenty meters of soil, then levels of hydrobags, support systems and storage and silage units, water and oxygen reclamation units, and microbiological "zoos." Plant growth is encouraged for aesthetic reasons and also to provide oxygen for station life support: IT IS THEREFORE IN YOUR INTEREST TO KEEP OFF THE GRASS.

Garden facilities include baseball

Zen Garden

Visiting Minbari dignitaries make frequent use of the Garden

The hedge maze

Down Below

SECURITY HOT SPOT. Located between the Garden and the hull, Down Below consists of several square kilometers of decks in which no new development has occurred due to financial cutbacks made by the Earth Alliance during station construction. Human and non-Human dropouts live here in shantytowns that are always moving. Illegal brothels, drug emporiums, and illegal medical facilities are to be found here. Down Below is an undeveloped area and may account for ninety percent of station crime. The inhabitants exist in an economy based mainly on barter. It is imperative that Security forces travel in squads. Food is scarce here. The unwary visitor may be killed and eaten as easily as mugged. Access is restricted to Security personnel and command staff. Public access is discouraged at any time.

Amos, a onetime resident

Garibaldi makes an arrest in Down Below

Ikaaran bioweapons may be found here

Invisibility-field suits in operation

Use of the Minbari fighting pike

Techno-mage sorcery: this group located themselves in Down Below

An agent of darkness caught in a Security trap

Garibaldi defends the station against unnamed invaders

Captain Sheridan is tested in an illegal facility

Incident during which Dr. Franklin is stabbed

5

unit 1

Unit 2: communications

A dequate communication is essential to public order and diplomatic policing, the main responsibilities of the Security Force on Babylon 5. Without it there can be no control and no way to command forces. In this unit we will look at all aspects of communication, including the types of electronic systems at our disposal, freight and cargo, and details on the Post Office, C&C (Command and Control), and the guilds.

2.1 COMMUNICATIONS– ELECTRONIC

D etailed below are the various means of communication among staff members on Babylon 5. Please note that it is essential that the correct codes be used at all times. Any abuse of these services can lead to disciplinary action.

Links

These are the hand-worn "PowerBooks™" and communication devices giving voice-only connections to the BabCom network. Each link holds several terabytes of personal and/or work-related information. Broadcast frequency is assigned automatically by the central computer. Operation is by voice command or by touch sensor (tapping the link). A voice mail service is available. Security staff members will be issued a link as part of basic training. Each link is encrypted with a personal molecular code. The link gives access to central computer facilities as well as Security areas within the station. Your link is your lifeline. With it you can be located anywhere in-station.

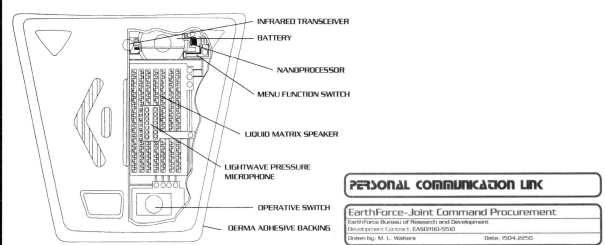

INFRARED TRANSCEIVER

BATTERY

NANOPROCESSOR

MENU FUNCTION SWITCH

LIQUID MATRIX SPEAKER

LIGHTWAVE PRESSURE MICROPHONE

OPERATIVE SWITCH

DERMA ADHESIVE BACKING

PERSONAL COMMUNICATION LINK

EarthForce-Joint Command Procurement
EarthForce Bureau of Research and Development
Development Contract: EASO/1110-5510

| Drawn by: M. L. Walters | Date: 1504.2250 |

BabCom

BabCom is the station's own communications network. A Galactel Matrix forms the internal central communications network of Babylon 5 and handles in-station, ship-to-shore, and ship-to-ship communications as well as links into StellarCom. BabCom carries 1,000 communication and educational channels. There are 2,300 monitors and viewscreens located throughout the station for public and private access.

BABCOM

StellarCom

StellarCom provides communications channels to all other systems within broadcast range of a jumpgate. Channels are assigned on a priority basis. For business and personal rates, check CenCom.

Gold Channel

This is the highest priority com-channel and is for official military use only. Access is via diplomatic card or security ident. Public use is limited to extreme emergencies, when all other com-channels are nonoperational. Monitoring use of Gold Channels to prevent misuse is essential to security. Monitoring content of Gold Channels is illegal, a breach of the Political Privacy Act of 2132, and therefore is punishable by military court-martial.

Personal Communication

In a personal emergency communication may be arranged at the discretion of your immediate superior.

Long-Range Communications

Long-range communications are effected via faster-than-light tachyon communicators. Ships emerging from hyperspace will notice a momentary loss of signal due to energy flux surrounding the jump point.

Babylon 5 Computer

The Babylon 5 computer has been upgraded to use the latest terran/alien hybrid silicon chip technology with laser read/write interface. Input to the fifteen-terabyte main database is via terminal, link, keyboard, or voice input. Response times vary between five and fifty picoseconds. Personality response is individually customizable. CenCom can handle up to 500,000 simultaneous complex functions in all languages. Processing time on language translation is currently down to 1.1 seconds. Data transfer is by crystal-silicon form.

Misuse of Gold Channel

"Don't. Not even if your father is dying."—MG

Emergency Communications

"I had this urgent call to make back home. My partner, you know, he was expecting the adoption order for our first child anytime. Anyway, most of the com-channels were down, and there was a lot of talk about the Narn-Centauri War flaring up, so I couldn't get through. I asked Mr. Garibaldi if he could do anything, and within a few hours he'd secured a line back home. By the way, it's a girl."
—Gavin Featherly, Security Officer

unit 2

Data Crystals

Data crystals are information storage and transport media used by most major races. Data crystals are available from a wide variety of sources. The main supplier is the Minbari race. Minbari crystals are individually coded via "Clay-RNA" to provide security and prevent counterfeiting. Data crystals are of uniform size—fifty gigabytes—although actual information size is dependent on the type of scanning medium. Their physical size is constant: 3.2 cm in length, conical, 1.2-cm base circumference.

Credit Chits

Credit chits will be needed to establish some lines of communication. Computer cards will keep track of your money (your salary will be tied to your credit chit). Visitors can exchange non-Earth currency at the Babylon 5 exchange. This is processed on the current rate of exchange and issued via credit chit. Anyone attempting to exchange cash illegally is to be arrested.

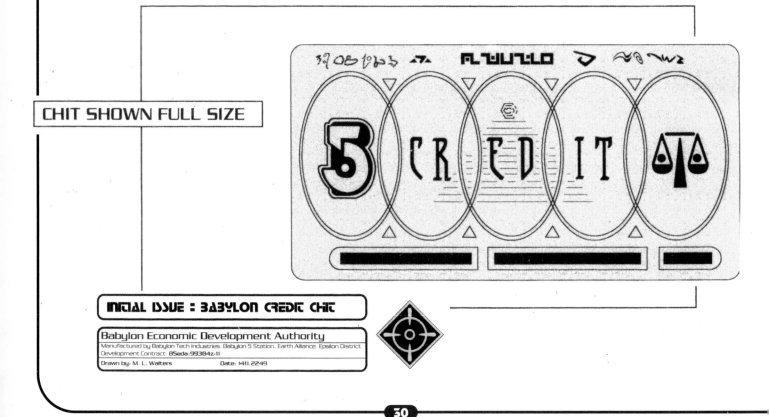

ENGRAVED HOLOGRAPHIC FACEPLATE

PROGRAMMABLE CRYSTAL MATRIX

NONCONDUCTING LAMINATE CASE

EMBEDDED CODE STRIP

CHIT SHOWN FULL SIZE

INITIAL ISSUE : BABYLON CREDIT CHIT

Babylon Economic Development Authority

Manufactured by Babylon Tech Industries. Babylon 5 Station. Earth Alliance. Epsilon District
Development Contract: B5eda:99384z-11

Drawn by: M. L. Walters   Date: 1411.2249

2.2 COMMUNICATIONS—FREIGHT & CARGO

When thinking of communications, the obvious means are link and BabCom. However, communications is a wider topic and also encompasses the various craft available on the station. Security has a main role to play in the transport areas, both internally and externally. It is here that potential trouble can first be spotted and averted, troublemakers detained, and illegal goods seized. In case of the seizure of illegally imported perishable goods—such as coffee and other luxury foodstuffs—the goods in question will be distributed according to priority assignments, usually to the Down Below aid stations or the officers' mess. R.H.I.P.

The Herschel *cargo ship*

Shuttles and Transport Craft

Babylon 5 is equipped with a fleet of zero-g Majestic Class transports. These disc-shaped models can carry two large cargo modules. Kneale Class cargo movers, which have two cargo racks on each side, are larger. These craft are quite old and travel relatively slowly. But they each mass more than eighty tons, so be sure to keep this in mind when policing the docks. Stop to sightsee, and the only sight you will see is the inside of medlab. Hammond Class crew transports carry twenty-five persons and have facilities for forty-eight hours of travel before reprovisioning. Top speed for these ships is .25 km/s. All ships smaller than the cruiser type require jumpgates or larger transports for intersystem travel. Sha'T'Nar Class transports have belly-space for up to 5,000 tons of freight and eight hundred passengers. Kestrel Class atmospheric shuttles are equipped with three ion engines and afterburners for maneuverability. Maximum linear thrust is 1 kps/ps. The standard crew numbers three.

The Patrick Moore *cargo ship*

The Skydancer *survey ship*

Ram Air Intakes

Cockpit

Static Ground Line

Profile

Particle Thrust Engine Module

Undercarriage Positions

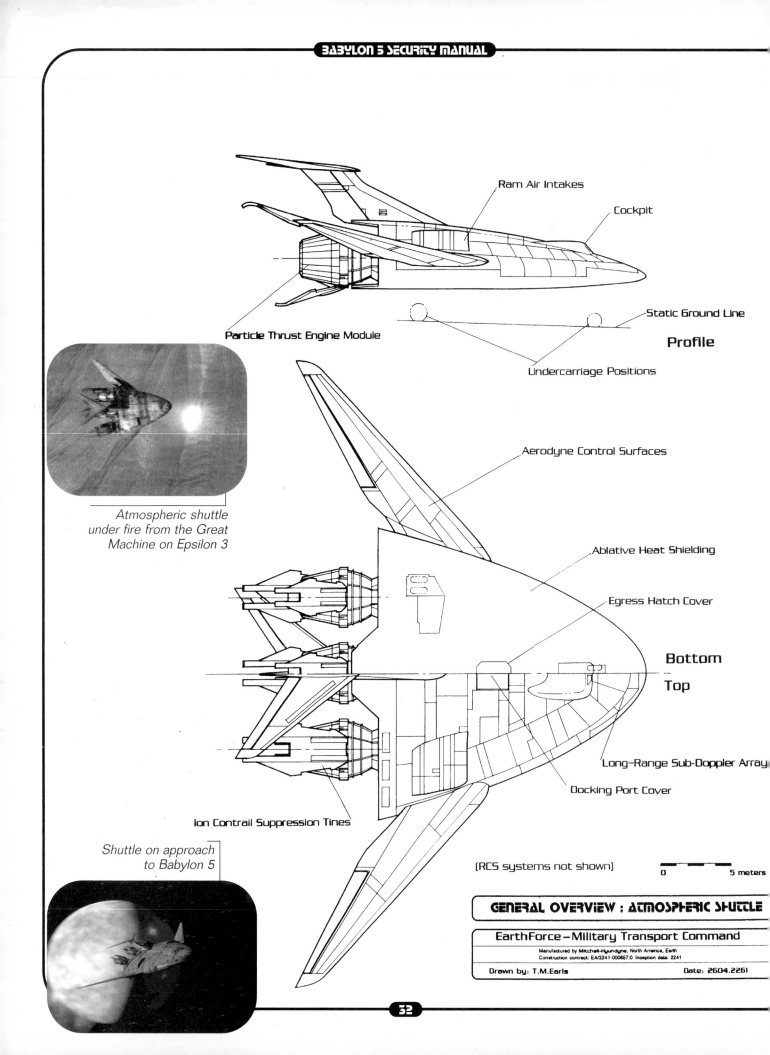

Atmospheric shuttle under fire from the Great Machine on Epsilon 3

Aerodyne Control Surfaces

Ablative Heat Shielding

Egress Hatch Cover

Bottom

Top

Long-Range Sub-Doppler Array

Docking Port Cover

Ion Contrail Suppression Tines

Shuttle on approach to Babylon 5

(RCS systems not shown)

0   5 meters

GENERAL OVERVIEW : ATMOSPHERIC SHUTTLE
EarthForce – Military Transport Command

Manufactured by Mitchell-Hyundyne, North America, Earth
Construction contract: EA/2241-000667:0 Inception date: 2241

Drawn by: T.M.Earls   Date: 2604.2261

Guilds

There are two main guilds relevant to this part of the station: the Transport Pilot Association (TPA) and the Dockers' Guild. The TPA is one of the many guilds onboard Babylon 5. Its symbol is a pair of silver wings over a gold disk. This guild is one of the more important on the station: it handles most transport and communications. The Dockers' Guild is by far the largest on the station. Members work mainly in the cargo area and cooperate fully with the Security squads. Initially, relations were strained between Babylon 5 and the Dockers' Guild, until Commander Sinclair smoothed over their grievances with EarthForce after the Rush Act had been invoked.

THE RUSH ACT

Dockers' Guild & the Rush Act

A typical example of how the Security forces can get entangled in situations is provided by the dockers' strike in 2259, when Babylon 5 still came under EarthForce jurisdiction. After a tragic accident in which a docker was killed, the guild demanded that all substandard and obsolete equipment be replaced. As there was no money available for this, a strike was called, initially using the cover of "illness." However, government contracts state that you cannot quit or strike until the term has expired, and so Earth sent in a hard-line labor negotiator who expected full cooperation from Security to provide troops if the Rush Act was invoked. After various negotiations broke down and against station advice, the Senate Labor Committee invoked the Rush Act—the first time since the New California strike on Europa in which more than a hundred people died.

The Rush Act basically enables the government to send in troops, remove and arrest strikers, and ship in new workers. Fortunately, Commander Sinclair had asked for the full text of the Senate order. After a riot had started involving the Security squad and the dockers in which morph gas was due to be used, Sinclair was empowered to end the strike "by any means necessary" and was given full support from the Earth representative. Sinclair resolved the crisis by reallocating 1.3 million credits from the military budget to buy new dock equipment and employ more personnel, besides offering complete amnesty to rioters unless any serious crimes had been committed and making sure that no charges were brought for fighting between Security and the Dockers' Guild.

Dock Worker/Security Force Relations

"Hey, man, some of my best friends are cops, right? Hell, my buddy Carlos is married to one! But we had to stick up for our rights, you know? That guy who died, you know, that wasn't good. You don't want that sorta thing happening to you. Anyway, it's all cool now: we go bowling with the guys on B Squad. They're okay."
—Uwe Seirts, Dock Worker

Vorlon ambassador Kosh rescues Sheridan from a near fatal Core Shuttle explosion

Core Shuttle & Transport Tube

See Unit 1 for details of the Core Shuttle and transport tubes. Note, however, that they can be overridden via the link in times of emergency; a good example of this occurred when a Centauri bomb was planted in the Core Shuttle to kill Captain Sheridan, who managed to override the door controls and jump out just before it blew up. To override the system, use your link to command the computer. This must be done only in emergencies. Authorization to do this is limited. Check your clearance codes.

If you are not cleared, you will need to contact C&C to gain override commands. In view of potential terrorist attacks, it is advised that you KEEP YOUR CODES WITH YOU AT ALL TIMES.

unit 2

Command and Control (C&C)

Command and Control is the center of station operations and communications. All systems can be accessed either directly or remotely from C&C. Gravity here is .3 g. C&C consists of five areas of operation:

i)   Environment

ii)   Jumpgate/navigational assistance

iii)   Security

iv)   Weaponry (defense grid)

v)   Sector surveillance

Only authorized staff members are allowed access to C&C

Technicians rotate in and out of this area on a regular basis. You should find at least one member of the command staff here at all times. Be aware that prolonged exposure to operations center work can result in mid- to high-level stress-related illness. Medlab staff monitor the C&C staff constantly for signs of psychological stress, but with two or three transports docking every minute, if anyone decides to go nuts, it is up to us to stop them.

There is an automatic self-maintenance system in operation with an alternating backup system (rotating every thirty to sixty minutes). Routine maintenance is fully logged with EC.

There is a backup C&C to handle the slow period of docking and overflow when the primary C&C is backed up.

Only authorized personnel are allowed in C&C. Public inspections are at the discretion of the captain only. Cameras and data recorders are strictly forbidden.

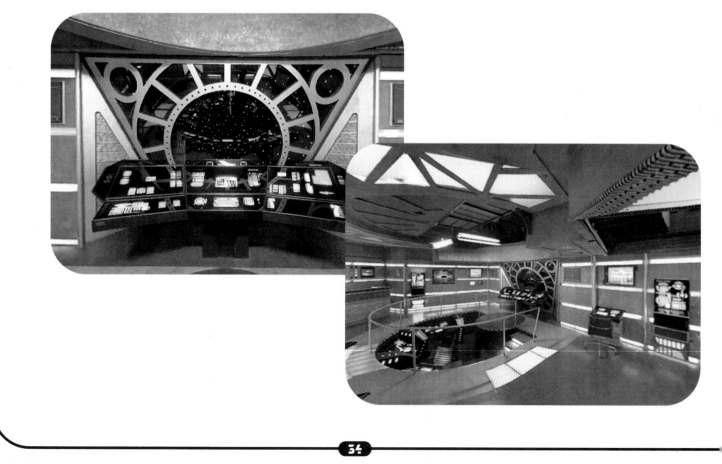

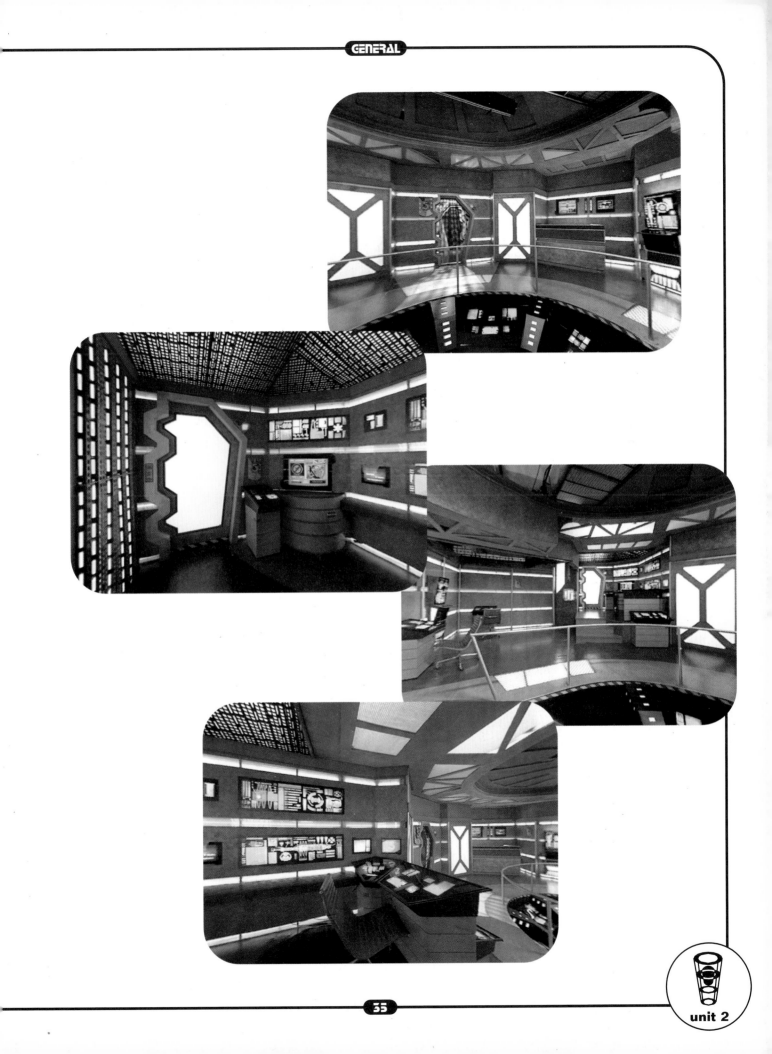

unit 2

Garibaldi at the Post Office

Post Office

"In my little corner of EarthForce the mail still gets delivered. If I got to use trap doors, alien transports, and back channels to get the mail in and out of here, then that's what I'll do . . ."
—Post Office Worker

Post Office

The Post Office is important to station life in terms of communications and morale. Communication with residents' homeworlds has become more difficult since the station seceded from the Earth Alliance. As a consequence, Security must be tightened regarding unclaimed items of mail. Post Office parcels therefore come under scrutiny from Customs (see Unit 3).

The break has also meant a change of name from the EarthForce Postal Service to simply the Postal Service. It has additionally meant an average threefold increase in transport charges.

The Post Office is closed for all major races' festivals and holidays (see separate list). It is worth noting that as with Earth holidays, the dates change slightly from year to year.

>>IMPORTANT INFORMATION<<
The Post Office Is Closed for the Following Festivals:

Earth

Jan. 1 & 2 (Western New Year), Jan. 12 (Sikh), Feb. 4–6 (Chinese New Year), Feb. 6 (Waitangi Day—New Zealand), March 17 (Irish), April 4 (Islamic), April 17–20 (Easter), April 25 (Anzac Day—Australia), May 4 (May Day), May 16 (Buddhist), May 25 (U.K. hol.), June 1 (Irish), June 4 (Sikh), June 7 (Jewish), June 11 (Islamic), June 23 (Portugal), July 1 (Islamic New Year and Canadian Dominion Day), July 4 (U.S. Independence Day), July 14 (Bastille Day), Aug. 21 (Hindu), Aug. 31 (U.K.), Sept. 1 (U.S. Labor Day), Sept. 9 (Islamic), Sept. 27 (Hindu), Sept. 28 (Jewish), Oct. 7 (Islamic), Oct. 12 (Jewish and Columbus Day,,Canada), Oct. 25 (Hindu), Nov. 15 (U.S. Thanksgiving), Nov. 23 (Fenric Day), Dec. 16 (Day of the Vow—South Africa), Dec. 20 (Jewish), Dec. 25–28 (Christian), Dec. 31 (Sikh)

EARTHFORCE POSTAL SERVICE

Centauri Prime

Jan. 13, Jan. 20, Jan. 26, Jan. 28, Feb. 7, Feb. 12, Feb. 26 (Sigma Day), Mar. 18, Mar. 23, April 1–3 (Fool's Festival), April 5, May 5, July 17 (Great Maker Festival), Sept. 14 (Koenig's Day), Sept. 15 (Dilgar War Remembrance), Dec. 28–Jan. 5 (Festival of Xon). Please note that the Centauri have fifty gods, all of which have a holiday (some on the same day). Only the dates are noted here. For further details please check the computer.

Minbar

Jan. 5–12 (Chudomo), Jan. 27 (Blag Day), May 30 (Valen Day), Sept. 15 (Dilgar War Remembrance), Dec. 3 (Markab Day of Remembrance)

Narn

Jan. 14–19 (G'Ukas), Feb. 1–3 (W'Nell), Feb. 16 (T'Bakas), March 6 (C'Bakas), April 11–12 (Na'Shok), May 12 (Festival of Boxing Lights/Centauri Liberation Day), May 17 (Day of Ellison), May 30–31 (P'M'Gon), Sept. 15 (Dilgar War Remembrance), Oct. 20–27 (G'Quan), Dec. 3 (Markab Day of Remembrance)

Non-Aligned Worlds

Most festivals or one-day holidays are celebrated by more than one world; please check computer logs for further information.

Jan. 21–25 (K'Bush), Jan. 29 (Prisoners Day), Jan. 30–31 (Festival of Forbidden Delights), Feb. 8–10 (Trow Tonne), Feb. 11 (J'Per'Ee), Feb. 13–15 (Last Ships of Tetrapania), Feb. 17–25 (Sons of Davi), Feb. 27–29 (Hogswatch), March 1–5 (Iolus's Many Meets), March 7 (McIntee's Find), March 8–16 (Eight-Day War Remembrance), March 18–20 (Smachoy), March 21–22 (Disney Planet Independence Celebration Festival), March 24–28 (Great Death Remembrance), March 27–31 (Pak'ma'ra Fasting & Solitude), April 6–10 (Shalos), April 13–16 (Survivors of M'Zen), April 21 (Officers' Day), April 22–24 (Officers' Day of Recovery), April 26–30 (Zabann), May 1–3 (Klatail), May 6 (O'Hare Day), May 7–11 (Sum of Klotha), May 13–15 (Blotast), May 18–24 (Drombarda), May 26–29 (Pratchettor), June 2–3 (Oflan), June 5–6 (Xonta), June 8–10 (Yncharson), June 12–15 (Welnip), June 16–22 (Oggwax), June 24–30 (Festival of the Four Winds), July 2 (Swazindee), July 3 (Humble Day), July 5–13 (Olyzes Lo), July 15–16 (Vantar), July 18–25 (Intosond), July 16–31 (Quontoba), Aug. 1–7 (Mistletas), Aug. 6–11 (Zast), Aug. 10–15 (Lotinda), Aug. 14–20 (Ertonda), Aug. 22–31 (J'Vondiz), Sept. 2–8 (Strakertz), Sept. 10–13 (Asdoput), Sept. 15 (Dilgar War Remembrance), Sept. 16–26 (Inchantzka), Sept. 29–30 (P'Tonta), Oct. 1–6 (Yvontis), Oct. 8–11 (N'Bo'No'Ti'Vi'Bo), Oct. 13–19 (Razta), Oct. 28–31 (Dkjfi), Nov. 1–14 (Jimindi), Nov. 16–22 (Forty Som'D), Nov. 24–30 (Utumbcz), Dec. 1–2 (S'Ts'Cmin), Dec. 3 (Markab Day of Remembrance), Dec. 4–9 (Wolves Are Running), Dec. 10 (Tall Men Remembrance), Dec. 17–19 (Baxters Ships), Dec. 21–24 (Finipee), Dec. 28–31 (Drazi Religious Festival)

Feb. 29 (Post Office Celebration of Work)

unit 2

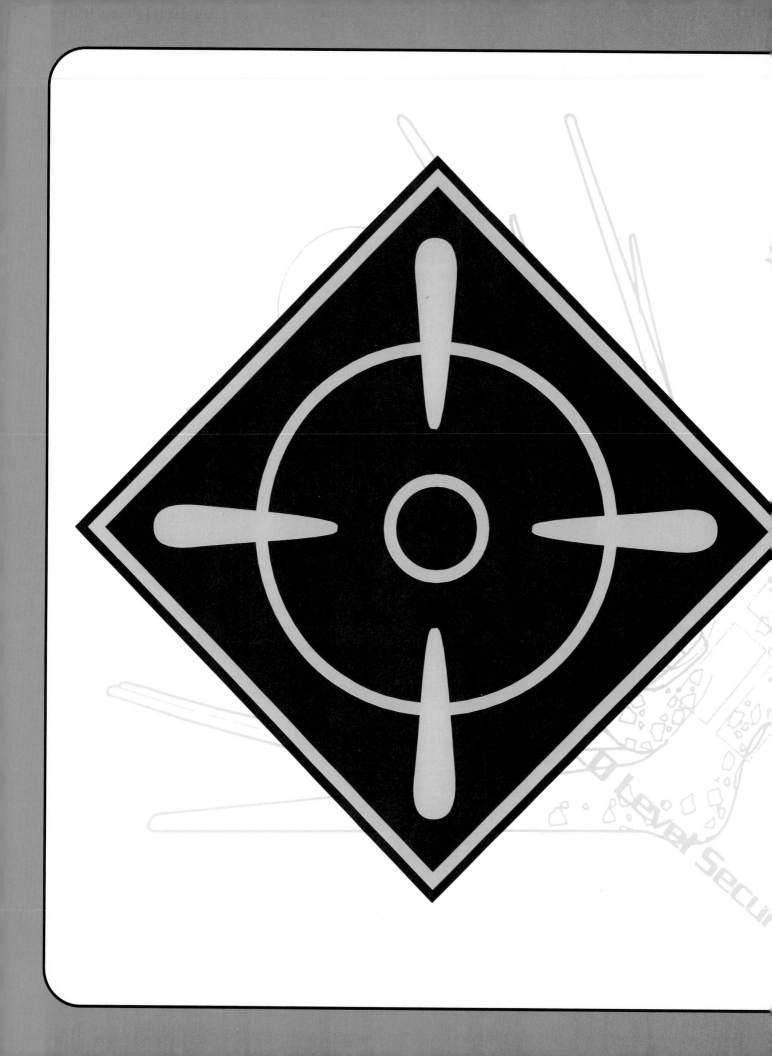

PART 2: SECURITY

3.1 A BRIEF HISTORY OF EARTHFORCE AND BABYLON 5

In this unit we will be looking at Security duties in more detail, finding out who we are and what we do. The role of Security on Babylon 5 will be discussed, and some case histories will be given. We will also take a look at the Customs Area and the Security aspects involved there.

It is helpful to understand the history behind the station and its ties with EarthForce in order to provide a background to these duties and explain in some way why the station works as it does.

It will help to think of Babylon 5 as a small colony or planet, at best a small city, with all the relevant problems that entails.

EarthForce

Before declaring independence, Babylon 5 came under the jurisdiction of the United Earth Military Force (EarthForce). As with other Earth colonies, such as those on Mars and Proxima 3, Babylon 5 was a governorship headed by a military official (Sinclair and then Sheridan).

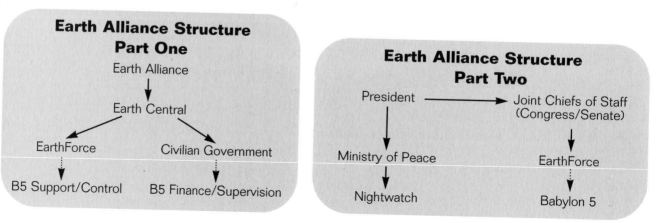

Earth Alliance Structure Part One

Earth Alliance → Earth Central → EarthForce → B5 Support/Control

Earth Central → Civilian Government → B5 Finance/Supervision

Earth Alliance Structure Part Two

President → Joint Chiefs of Staff (Congress/Senate)

President → Ministry of Peace → Nightwatch

Joint Chiefs of Staff → EarthForce → Babylon 5

Since the station's secession and declaration of itself as an independent state, the basic structure has changed little. The most noticeable changes are the removal of the Babylon 5 Council–Earth Senate link and the threefold increase in trading charges.

With the break from Earth, the split in the Minbari Grey Council, and the onset of the Shadow War, Babylon 5 has had to become more and more independent. One example of this is the inclusion of Narn forces in the Security staff. This was done after members of Nightwatch were thrown out of the Security service and deported from the station.

Before being overthrown by Sheridan's liberation forces, President Clark issued several decrees that reconstituted the Senate Committee on Anti-Earth Activities, with powers linked to Psi Corps, which had become more important in the new order on Earth. The Psi Corps still holds much power and is certain to cause more conflict in the power structure in the years to come.

How We Got Here

1960s The first probes are sent into space. The manned spaceflight program culminates in Neil Armstrong becoming the first man to set foot on the surface of the moon.

1980s The first reusable spaceship (Space Shuttle) is built.

1997 The first official acknowledgment of life on other planets is made, bringing forward manned flights to Mars and the building of space stations and moon bases.

1999 The United States president, Bill Clinton, forms the President's Commission on the Future.

2018 The foundation is laid for the first lunar colony in the Sea of Tranquillity.

2075–2170 A period of exploration and colonization within our own system sees the inception of the Mars, moon, and Io colonies. Generation ships are launched beyond the solar system, and the countries of the world "unite" as Earth Central.

2161 Psi Corps is created.

2184 First contact with the Centauri. There is a major influx of alien spacefaring technology and cultural and scientific exchanges. Humanity leapfrogs two hundred years in terms of technology and finally achieves interstellar travel capability. Initially the Centauri claim that Earth is a lost Centauri colony, but this is later found to be untrue.

The Babylon 5 Treaty

You may in the course of your duties hear mention of the Babylon 5 Treaty. This was a document drafted by ourselves to provide protection to the station after pulling away from Earth. The Babylon 5 Treaty was drawn up by representatives of Minbar and the League of Non-Aligned Worlds to provide an ongoing defense of Babylon 5 and also to provide interworld cooperation in defense matters. It proved valuable during the recent Shadow War.

2230 First contact with the Narn. A refugee from the aftermath of the first Narn-Centauri War brings word of Centauri atrocities.

2243 First contact with the Minbari. A cultural misunderstanding brings about the first conflict.

2244 The Earth-Minbari war begins.

2247 Minbari forces surrender without explanation on the verge of victory.

2250–2254 The Babylon Project is initiated in a response to the Earth-Minbari War. Babylons 1–3 are sabotaged, and the fourth vanishes twenty-four hours after going on-line.

2254–2256 Babylon 5 is constructed.

2257 First contact is established with the Vorlons. Third Age of Mankind begins.

unit 3

5.2 RULES & REGULATIONS

Security

As a representative of the Security Services on Babylon 5, you must maintain good conduct at all times. We operate under a policy of containment, not confrontation. SOP is, whenever possible, to contain the incident before attempting a resolution. Only in major disturbances will a "raid group" storm the area. In these major incidents you may be required to join colleagues in a search of the premises if there has been no contact with perpetrators. Elite weaponry squads are on around-the-clock callout, but you may be required to make shoot/no shoot decisions yourself, as illustrated in training.

In your training you will experience realistic security simulations, for example, Scenario Fifteen, in which an armed person barricades himself and a number of hostages in a room. (The object is to retrieve the hostages unharmed and the kidnapper alive if possible.)

Training will include methods of dealing with an armed person or persons, modes of restraint, removal from civilian vicinity, and provision for maximum self/civilian preservation.

The outcome of given circustances is determined by split-second decisions. Learn to make good ones: lives depend on them, not the least of which is probably your own.

You will get regular refresher training and the opportunity to obtain advanced training, including ambassadorial protection and the use of multiple weapons against single/multiple targets.

The Security Services on Babylon 5 Have Certain Powers:

Ø Powers to stop and search for a variety of offenses, including stolen or prohibited articles.

Ø Powers relating to entry, search, and seizure.

Ø Powers of arrest, with and without a warrant.

Ø Powers to detain and question (period of detention before arrest is limited in relation to the crime being investigated).

Ø Powers to obtain evidence relating to crimes (e.g., prints, stomach contents, body samples).

Ø Powers to limit access to sensitive areas.

It is due to the wide range of areas covered that you may find yourself stationed in Customs for a few days before being moved on to crowd control, shoplifting patrols, ambassadorial protection, or even the Emergency War/Attack Squad on callout.

There are various safeguards in place to prevent "overenthusiasm in the pursuit of duties," including supervision and complaints procedures. There are specified procedures for supervision, necessary grounds for action, and codes of conduct.

These Rest on Three Basic Principles:

- Ø Making a suspect's rights clear and known and making police powers unambiguous.
- Ø Making a clear line of responsibility for actions, including the welfare of suspects being held.
- Ø Making clear and comprehensive records, which will be made available when needed both to the suspect and to the authorities.

Anyone is entitled to make a complaint about the Security on Babylon 5, be it a general complaint or one specifically relating to an individual or incident.

Complaints made are logged on to the station computer and passed to the chief of Security and the station commander. Each is considered individually, and the necessary action is taken.

No one is above the law.

Earth Alliance laws and regulations have been adopted on Babylon 5. The station operates as an independent state, and the Earth Senate is no longer involved in policy decisions or the day-to-day running of the station. These matters are now referred to either the Babylon 5 Committee or one of its subcommittees.

As well as all the usual laws and crime situations, Security has to enforce license-holding laws (for traders, etc.) and make sure that the religious institutions on the station apply for the correct status (e.g., monks on the station must hold a Missionary License of Class C-10 or above).

Security

"The unauthorized use of official information is the worst fault a Security officer can commit. It is on the same footing as cowardice by a soldier. It is unprofessional and can be extremely dangerous!"
—Jonathan Cooper,
Security Disciplinary Officer

Rules

There are various rules and regulations on the station (see companion volume *Rules and Regulations—Their Adaptation from EA Rules and Use on Babylon 5*). You will have full training in this area, but the following lists the main points to remember, including case notes.

The usual crimes you will face include robbery, murder, rape, theft, and mugging. (Correct call codes should be used—see Appendix 1.) Remember, the station is a free port, a place of commerce, trade, and diplomacy for all species, and so legal situations can be tricky. The commander of Babylon 5 used to have authority to speak on behalf of Earth, the same as a ship's captain exploring new worlds, on an equal footing with alien ambassadors. This is no longer the case.

Ø There should be no firearms on the station except for EarthForce and Security (there are exceptions, such as Rangers and war situations).

Ø No drugs on Babylon 5 that are not strictly medicinal.

Ø No unlicensed telepaths operating as adjuncts to business contracts.

Ø Kidnapping is treated as a serious offense. (Maximum force had to be used on one occasion against a race known as the Streibs, who take subjects for testing to determine whether their races are a threat. In this case they abducted Captain Sheridan.)

Ø It is forbidden to use the station's personnel or firepower as a threat to force someone to sign a particular treaty. It would be counted as duress and nullify the contract.

Consult your EarthForce regulations and acts passed for further details. There are only three acts so far that are not recognized on the station: Capital Punishment by Means of Spacing, the Rush Act, and the Sunday Trading Rules (all of which have been declared immoral). The rules on mindwiping are currently being examined. (See under "Crime and Punishment," below.)

Rush Act—Further Details

Please see details of the Rush Act in the previous unit. The law refers only to unions and is not a wide-ranging piece of legislation. Earth law enables the Senate to empower an authorized agent to end an illegal strike by using "any means necessary," which usually results in the use of force.

"Implementation of the Rush Act has so far resulted in 403 deaths, including two prematurely terminated births, seventy-eight casualties, and one seriously angry Security chief. A month after the fact I had to jail two mothers on three counts of assault and murder one.
It's worse than a posse of rock jockeys striking uranium. It can ruin your whole day."—MG

Originally developed during the Earth-Minbari War to deal with noncooperative union or corporation factions, the Rush Act has been declared immoral as well as an incitement to riot and is not enforced on Babylon 5.

3.3 CRIME & PUNISHMENT

Babylon 5 has its own court and resident judges. There are various punishments, which include the usual compensation payments, fines, seizure of goods, imprisonment, extradition, banishment from the station, and mindwiping.

As capital punishment, spacing is no longer accepted; other sentencing is now passed for acts of mutiny or treason. Mindwiping (sometimes referred to as "death of personality") is the removal of a person's memory as punishment for a crime. The person concerned must be scanned before and after by a licensed telepath to confirm that the procedure has been successful.

Opinion on the procedure is divided: some consider the sentence more humane than the death penalty, while others contend that "death of personality" is in fact an immoral crime in its own right.

There is evidence to suggest that the procedure is not permanent in all cases and that old memories can remain in some form, resulting in various forms of personality disorders.

The equipment to perform a mindwipe is kept in a high-security vault in medlab and is released only upon a mandate from the court. The templates to replace memories with others or with variations also are kept locked away.

After mindwipe an ex-criminal is moved away from the area of the crime. The criminal's civil rights are also restricted. This process is monitored by the New Man Support Agency, an institution set up and funded via public taxes. Lately, a huge debate has been raging about the use to which public money has been put in the matter of supporting and sometimes even improving the quality of life of convicted murderers and rapists.

Ombuds

Ombuds Wellington and Ombuds Zimmerman were the legal adjudicators for the Earth Alliance on the station. Since the secession, both judges have allowed their job functions to become privatized. They now accept fees, which are generally set on a case-by-case basis. Legal aid is assigned only rarely in the limited financial framework now extant on the station.

Ombuds Case

Ombuds Wellington often is heard saying that he gets the more unusual cases. As is the law, all legal proceedings have to be heard.

One case that attracted a lot of interest was the accusation against a Vree (also referred to as a "Grey"), which was finally resolved on October 13, 2258. The case involved the abduction of an ancestor of a Human.

It was alleged that in the late twentieth century the ancestor of David Anderson, a law enforcement agent, was abducted while carrying out his duties by an ancestor of Crck'Artor, a Vree. The Vree admitted that the abduction was carried out, and an official apology was offered.

A groundbreaking closing speech uncovered the truth behind the famous abductions of the twentieth and twenty-first centuries, and damages were ordered, paving the way for more cases against the Vree over the next year.

Ombuds Wellington

3.4 NONTERRESTRIAL CRIME

Ombuds are empowered to use their own discretion with regard to crimes committed by non-Humans while on-station. The war criminal Jha'dur, for instance, escaped station law when a series of governments (including Earth) stepped in. This was not for legitimate reasons. Jha'dur was a war criminal who had found the secret of immortality and intended to release a (gene-corrupted) version into the public health sector. In an unprecedented example of supreme responsibility, the Vorlon government simply killed Jha'dur by destroying her spaceship. Quasi-sentient predatory animals such as the Na'ka'leen feeder are expressly forbidden on all planets where intelligent life exists to be psychically preyed on. The Drazi have a ceremony in which they each pick a colored sash from a bag, either green or purple. They then proceed to fight among themselves. When this happened on the station, the fighters were held until the problem was resolved.

Persons to Watch

Desmond Mosechenko (aka Deuce)

A violent extortionist who escaped from custody off-station after being brought to justice. He brought a Na'ka'leen feeder onboard and used it as a weapon of blackmail.

Junior (real name unknown)

Guilty of subversive activities against the smooth running of station activity. It is alleged that some of his goods are fake and that he has caused endless legal problems for most of his business associates. (Any evidence is being kept confidential until the trial.)

You can download pictures of these and other wanted creatures from the computer.

Customs

If you are posted to the Customs Area, you should wear a name badge as well as your identicard and link, etc.

You should offer to help repack bags if you have unpacked them while searching for contraband items. All straightforward claims should be referred to the Customs staff, which should settle them within ten working days.

If you need to do a search, you should mention the rights of the individual and the reason for the search (whether routine or due to suspicions). In tandem with this, you also should be conversant with duty and tax as you will no doubt have to explain this at some point (if taking money, also remember to give a receipt).

If there are any delays in Customs, report it to C&C immediately and also give the reason on the computers to the public. You will also need to be aware of procedure regarding complaints and adjudicators.

Your role is to prevent the importation of illegal items. These prohibited goods are mainly drugs, weapons, and obscene materials that pose a threat either to the physical or to the moral well-being of station residents.

We can check any travelers and their ships to see if they are smuggling drugs and other goods, though you must try to cause as little trouble and delay as possible when doing your job.

You must treat all races fairly, respecting their rights and explaining those rights to them. The law of the station is on your side if you decide a search is needed; however, you must take care not to damage anything.

Duty and tax can be paid in credit chits, by credit transfers, by any recognized form of currency, by data crystal, or by other forms of barterable goods (see list in the Customs Area).

There are certain ships and traders to be on the lookout for. Always update yourself when entering Customs and refer to the following lists regarding important ships and banned items.

The only exception to all these rules is the Vorlon race, which has unlimited access without the usual Customs rules. You will know the Vorlons by their unique encounter suits, full details of which can be found on the computer.

Prohibited Goods

Besides the usual items, the following goods are banned on-station:

Ø Bab-bear-lon 5 bears and associated merchandise

Ø Centauri figures without personal "appendages" (manufacture of licensed "appendaged" facsimiles is permitted subject to a copyright tax payable directly to the Centauri ambassador)

Ø Lumati sex toys

Ø Certain Old Calendar "TeeVee" programs, including *The X-Files* (considered "offensively truthful" by the Vree race) and *Absolutely Fabulous* (considered offensive by more than fifty-eight different species) but excluding Warner Bros. cartoons and Lumati educational films (considered wholesome and stimulating by every alien race—particularly the Lumati)

Ø Clavundi (except on the seventeenth day of the fourth month of every year whose date forms a palindrome)

Ø Fluffy dice (navigation hazard when used in Starfury cockpits)

Ø Live yogurt (dead yogurt is permitted)

Ø Centauri opera—banned by Narn

Ø Narn opera—banned by Centauri

Ø Certain literature (The Dark Tide, P'Van Zat, Ze Dit & Zeepeededooda)

Ø Certain music (anything by the following—The Destructors, Disaster Area, Anthony Newley, Cwif Wichodd, Have This, J'otef Loch & The Space Niverls)

Lumati d'Uhmfruit

An example of problems caused when Customs procedure is not followed is the Lumati d'Uhmfruit. This small orange fruit looks harmless but was banned on Traken 5 when it destroyed the ozone layer there after having been imported for only a couple of days. A couple of these were let through Customs and were responsible for the death of two people in the quarters of Officer Tony Tyler, who escaped with only minor burns. The fruit causes a buildup of noxious gas that can suffocate and is highly flammable.

"I was on my way to see Dud when I heard the sound of muffled screams. Dud was lucky—it took environmental control technicians four hours to normalize the atmosphere in his quarters."—Professor Glenn Reed, Lycanthropological Studies

So far we have looked at Security as a whole and its part in the overall setup on Babylon 5—its duties and the roles you should expect to fill.

In this unit we will start by looking more closely at the way Security is set up, the chain of command on the station, uniforms, and equipment. We will also take a look at accident and emergency services as well as disease risks and prevention.

4.1 SECURITY ORGANOGRAM

In this section we will see how the Security Department fits into the overall running of Babylon 5.

Uniform

The uniforms on the station have changed a few times since we went on-line (due to the breakaway from Earth, the war, etc.). Full schematics on the uniforms can be downloaded from the computer. You will be expected to be familiar with these.

The basic uniform jacket has leather on the right front panel, collar, and cuffs, although some tunics do not have leather at all. There are bronze clamps and belt clasps at the base of the jacket, which can be worn open.

The shirt will have a logo on it, and you will also notice a general patch on the left shoulder (e.g., a Starfury patch) and a unit badge on the right. An EA command patch with your name on it is worn on the left breast (and, where appropriate, any off-world patch).

Command staff members, such as the chief of Security, wear a mainly black uniform given as a gift by the Minbari. It is made of various materials. The stitching on the front panel is Zirka thread. Zirka thread is derived from a rare Minbari plant; the inclusion of it in a gift of clothing is a rare honor. Zirka thread produces a mild allergic reaction in eighty percent of Humans. Due to cutbacks in the system, officers will be expected to pay for the fitting and upkeep of their own uniforms.

The dress uniform has no leather on the jacket panel. Variations include silver piping on jacket sleeves.

The combat uniform is worn beneath a grey or black flak jacket designed to deflect and dissipate the impact of energy weapons.

Dress Code

"I feel like I'm wearing a damn tent."
—Zack Allan,
Chief of Security

Uniform Colors

Blue ....EarthForce space forces
Green/brown ....EarthForce Marines (surface division)
Grey ....Security officers
Charcoal ....Medical
Light grey ....Prison
Black ....Psi Corps
Yellow.................Station techs, maintenance crews (not part of the EA)

The Earth Alliance symbol (EA command badge/patch) is a stylized EA in silhouette, and then altered within the lines to accommodate different divisions— Command has crosshatching, Security a gun sight, and technicians (electricians) a lightning strike. These are worn on the left chest, directly over the stat bar.

Stat Bars

These are bars of colored metal worn beneath the EA badge on the left breast. The color indicates the "status" of the wearer, not the rank (which is indicated by bars on the epaulettes).

Gold ....Command
Silver ....Command staff
Silver/gold...........Station executive officer (second in command)
Red ....Medical
Green ....Security
Yellow.................Sciences
Blue ....Pilots

Also on the right shoulder of Starfury squad members is a winged planet emblem, a five-pointed command insignia circled by red and gold and overlaid with gold wings over the pilot's name.

You will be expected to remember the following ranks in the station, denoted by their badges:

General (joint chiefs).........Five "stars" in a circle
General............................Polygon, one bronze bar, two stylized stars
Colonel............................Silver bird
Major ....Three diamond shapes
Captain ....Two diamond shapes
Lieutenant........................One diamond shape
Chief warrant officer ....One diamond shape with oblique black stripe areas
Admiral ....Polygon and three bronze stars
Captain ....Polygon and two bronze stars
Commander......................Polygon and one bronze star
Lieutenant Commander ......Polygon and one silver bar
Ensign.............................Bronze star

Command Staff

Commander
Captain Sheridan
(previously Commander Sinclair)

Chief of Security
Zack Allan
(previously M. Garibaldi)

↓

Security/Intelligence/
Surveillance/Customs

Second in Command
Susan Ivanova

↓

C&C

Station Doctor
Stephen Franklin

↓

Medlab

unit 4

4.2 SECURITY CENTRAL

Security Central is the place where the various aspects of security are coordinated. It is the center for surveillance on the station. From there the station sensors can be hooked into the Security system. Duty officers monitor constantly for unauthorized discharges from PPG weapons.

Infrared, ultraviolet, and normal-wavelength cameras are situated throughout the station. There are also the disk-shaped cambots, which can move around and record independently or to set programs. Cambots also are available in a handheld or gun-mounted format. Access can also be gained to the maintenance 'bots operating outside the station (see also pages 80–81).

Nightwatch takes control

Securebots with securecams are also outside the station with cameras that have full pan (360 degrees on all axes) and full zoom (to optical limit) and are operable by zone or in groups.

All cells have monitors, and every habitation room on the station can be accessed through the BabCom system. The monitors in the cells can be important for a number of reasons.

In one instance we had the infamous Mr. Morden in custody. The monitors were used to scan different wavelengths, and the Shadow creatures accompanying him showed up on the screen; this convinced Sheridan that holding Mr. Morden at that time was inadvisable.

Mr. Morden proved to be a Shadow ally

Life on the Firing Line

"You wouldn't believe some of the things you see out in the Big Dark. Beer cans, desiccated sandwiches . . . Cleanup patrol's a bummer, man. Except that I saw the Shadows when they surrounded the station that time . . . that was scary, I can tell you. I even saw a teddy bear once, though I'd lay long odds you won't believe me."
—Clive Evans, Pilot, First Class

4.3 PERSONAL SECURITY EQUIPMENT

This section will deal with the various items of equipment that are part of your lives as Security operatives.

PPG

The phased plasma gun fires a "bolt" that is an extremely hot charge of energized helium (plasma) in a magnetic containment field. This is propelled by an electrical charge. The field dissipates upon impact with a solid object, leaving the plasma charge to react directly with the target. Displacement of supercharged air molecules results in the characteristic "thunderclap" sound heard on discharge.

The plasma bolt is able to cut through flesh and thin metal (it does not ricochet apart from metals specially coated for further protection, such as certain blast doors).

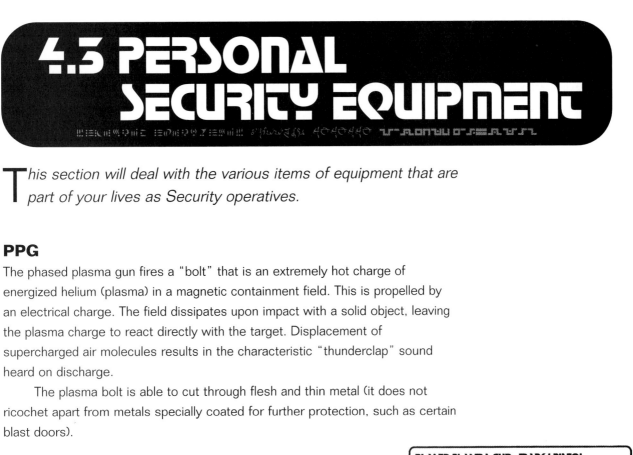

PHASED PLASMA GUN : MARK I PISTOL
Earth Force - Security Division Procurement
Earth Force Weapons Research and Development Command
Development Contract. EASO/9091-7782:A
Drawn by: M. L. Walters   Date: 3004.2240

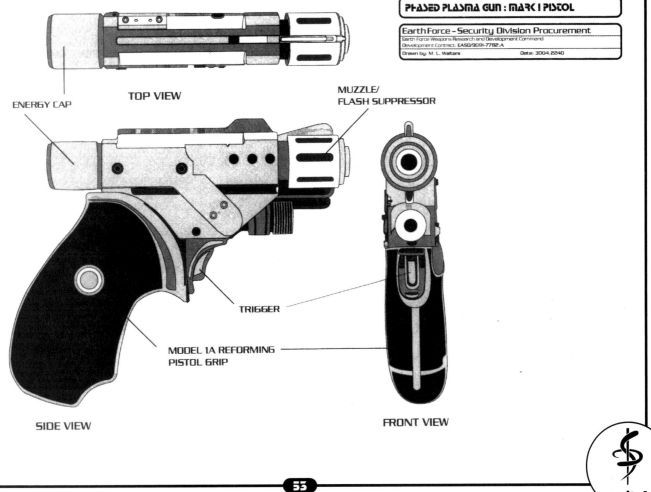

ENERGY CAP

TOP VIEW

MUZZLE/
FLASH SUPPRESSOR

TRIGGER

MODEL 1A REFORMING
PISTOL GRIP

SIDE VIEW

FRONT VIEW

There are three PPG settings:

1 This will produce a solid impact without significant burning.

2 This burst will produce surface damage.

3 This setting will burn into a body, causing damage to skin and muscle and, if used continuously, severe damage to internal tissue and bones.

Even at the lowest setting continuous use can cause serious burns and self-cauterization of wounds and melt clothes to the skin.

PPGs come in side holsters and are designed for a quick draw. PPGs weigh less than your lunchbox and are easy to miss, so beware of pickpockets while on patrol. The safety control is located at the thumb position on the handgrip for easy access. The arming process takes 0.003478 of a second.

Cadet Jason DiNalt shot three people by accident because he was not familiar with the hair-trigger responses of the well-designed PPG. Remember: your PPG is your best buddy. You look after him, he'll look after you. Neglect him and watch out!

Magazine pods hold twelve rounds. The trigger discharges stored energy, and every magazine is good for four to twelve shots. The number of shots differs depending on the setting:

1 Low—twelve shots

2 Standard—seven shots

3 High—four shots

The serial number of each weapon is found on the nearly indestructible morbidium core. If there is not a serial number on the weapon, it is more than likely one belonging to Special Forces.

PPG Rifle

The PPG rifle is a much larger weapon and has a built-in laser sight. It can recharge and fire twice as quickly as a normal PPG pistol. Magazines hold up to twenty-four shots.

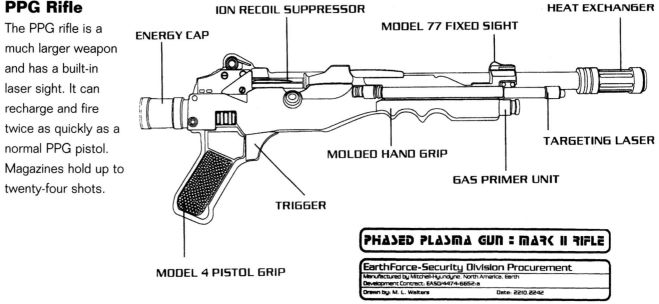

ENERGY CAP

ION RECOIL SUPPRESSOR

MODEL 77 FIXED SIGHT

HEAT EXCHANGER

MOLDED HAND GRIP

TARGETING LASER

GAS PRIMER UNIT

TRIGGER

MODEL 4 PISTOL GRIP

PHASED PLASMA GUN : MARK II RIFLE

EarthForce-Security Division Procurement
Manufactured by Mitchell-Hyundyne. North America. Earth
Development Contract: EASD/4474-6652:a
Drawn by: M. L. Walters   Date: 2210.2242

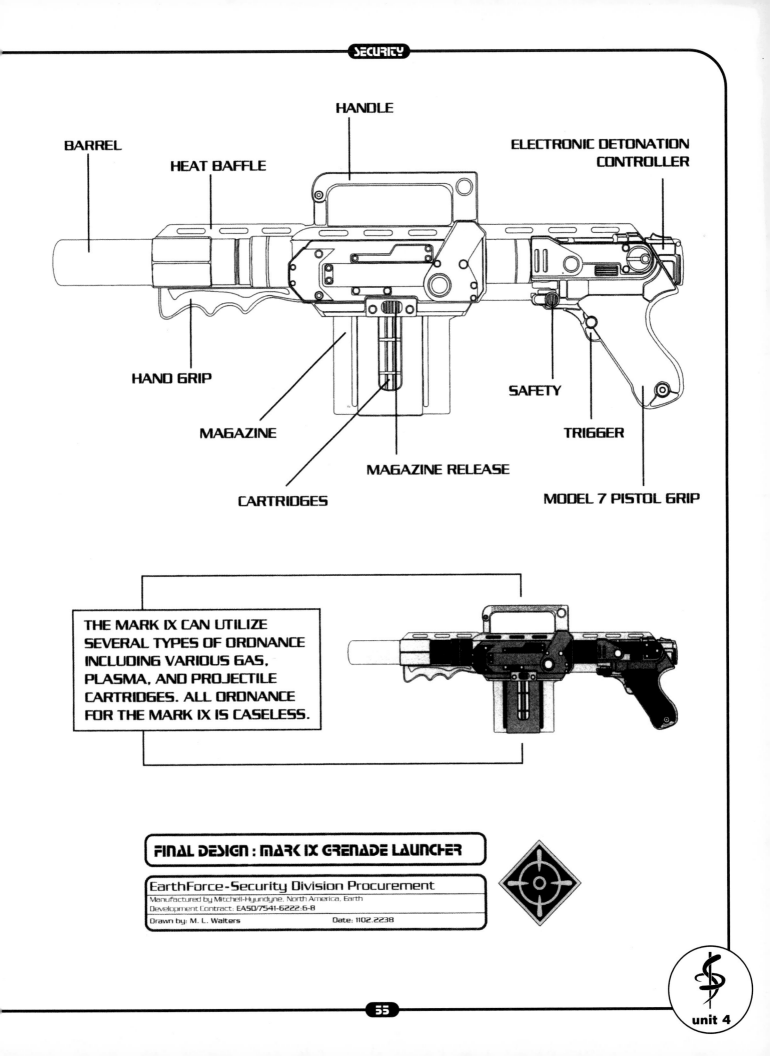

BARREL

HEAT BAFFLE

HANDLE

ELECTRONIC DETONATION CONTROLLER

HAND GRIP

MAGAZINE

CARTRIDGES

MAGAZINE RELEASE

SAFETY

TRIGGER

MODEL 7 PISTOL GRIP

THE MARK IX CAN UTILIZE
SEVERAL TYPES OF ORDNANCE
INCLUDING VARIOUS GAS,
PLASMA, AND PROJECTILE
CARTRIDGES. ALL ORDNANCE
FOR THE MARK IX IS CASELESS.

FINAL DESIGN : MARK IX GRENADE LAUNCHER

EarthForce-Security Division Procurement
Manufactured by Mitchell-Hyundyne, North America, Earth
Development Contract: EASD/7541-6222:6-8

Drawn by: M. L. Walters   Date: 1102.2238

unit 4

Shock Sticks

Shock sticks interfere with the nerve signals in the body and can disable a person quite easily. They are long baton-shaped sticks and need recharging after twenty shocks. Although far "safer" than the old truncheons, they can inflict serious injuries that may need medical attention.

This weapon is ideal against members of violent crowds and has been invaluable in riot situations.

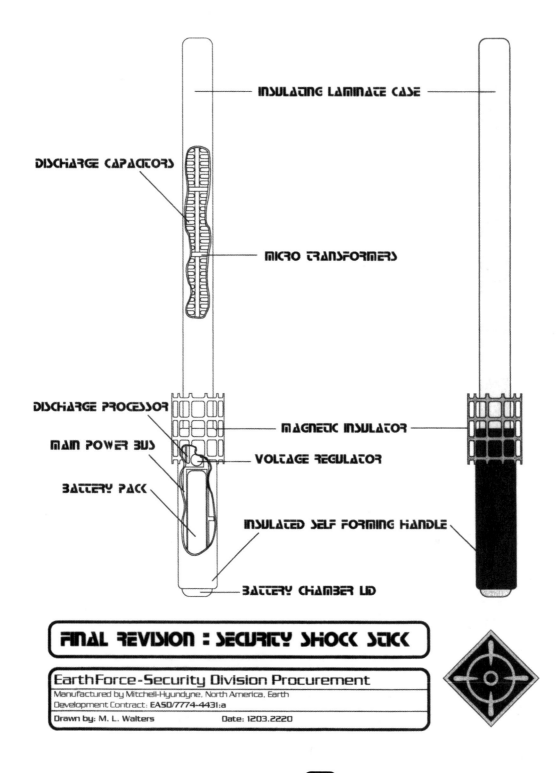

INSULATING LAMINATE CASE

DISCHARGE CAPACITORS

MICRO TRANSFORMERS

DISCHARGE PROCESSOR

MAGNETIC INSULATOR

MAIN POWER BUS

VOLTAGE REGULATOR

BATTERY PACK

INSULATED SELF FORMING HANDLE

BATTERY CHAMBER LID

FINAL REVISION : SECURITY SHOCK STICK

EarthForce-Security Division Procurement

Manufactured by Mitchell-Hyundyne, North America, Earth
Development Contract: EASD/7774-4431:a

Drawn by: M. L. Walters   Date: 1203.2220

Riot Gear

Riot gear really consists of protective additions to other weapons rather than further equipment. When on riot duty, you will be given a flak jacket, the equivalent of a bulletproof vest, which can absorb or reflect most moderate-level PPG blasts. This does not mean that risks can be taken, as the vests do not last long. However, heavy-duty personal armor is available when the conflict looks to be major in scope or duration. Appropriate headgear is also issued.

Use of Weapons

"We had to quell a few riots on the station, but it was all handled with no problems, as the weapons really did their job. They are quite easy to handle when you get used to them."
—Nigel Webster, Security Officer

"Weapons can have different effects on different races. I was one of the squad called in to kill the Vorlon, and I'll never forget it. They take a lot of killing, and if it wasn't for Sheridan and the old Kosh, I don't know what we'd have done."
—Steve Lunn, Security Officer

Riot gear in use

unit 4

Morph Gas

If violence is not being contained by means of dispersal tactics employing shock sticks and PPGs, the next step is to use morph gas. This is an anesthetic gas used to quell riots. Effectiveness is limited to Human and near-Human metabolisms. Humans, Centauri, and Grome are affected easily, but it takes longer with Narn and Pak'ma'ra.

Sleepers

Not really a weapon, sleepers are drugs used by Psi Corps to repress telepathic abilities in those who will not join the Corps. The drugs may be used against Psi Corps operatives if the need arises.

Star Webbing

Star webbing is energized webbing used to immobilize or incapacitate a person. However, it is somewhat clumsy and is not used to a great extent.

4.4 CELLS

There are thirty cells, split into those capable of holding individuals and those used for larger numbers. Containment is via matrix shielding. Toilet facilities, once standard, were removed after an incident in which overcrowding meant that a Cauralline was imprisoned in a Human holding cell (see Unit 4.7 "Toilet Facilities").

Since the secession, space on Babylon 5 is at a premium, so it is policy to avoid using cells whenever possible.

Personal Hygiene

"The Cauralline are a newly contacted species, so we didn't know that the chemical sterilizer in the urinal was a slow poison to Cauralline physiology. Of course we know that now, and steps have been taken to avoid similar tragedies, but there was hell to pay at the time. The Cauralline in question took three days to die; he was only in prison awaiting trial for petty shoplifting."
—Stephen Franklin, Chief Medical Officer

4.5 IDENTICARDS

Identicards are a combination of a credit card and an identity card but are also used for passports, personal calendars, and medical files (all information is contained on a memory crystal similar to those in the station computer).

   DNA records are also held on the card, making important identification situations virtually foolproof.

   This does not mean that criminals cannot get around the system, as proved by Del Varner onboard Babylon 5 in 2258, when he died in the process of selling outlawed alien technology. Others known to have gotten around the system include Mr. Morden (probably using Shadow technology).

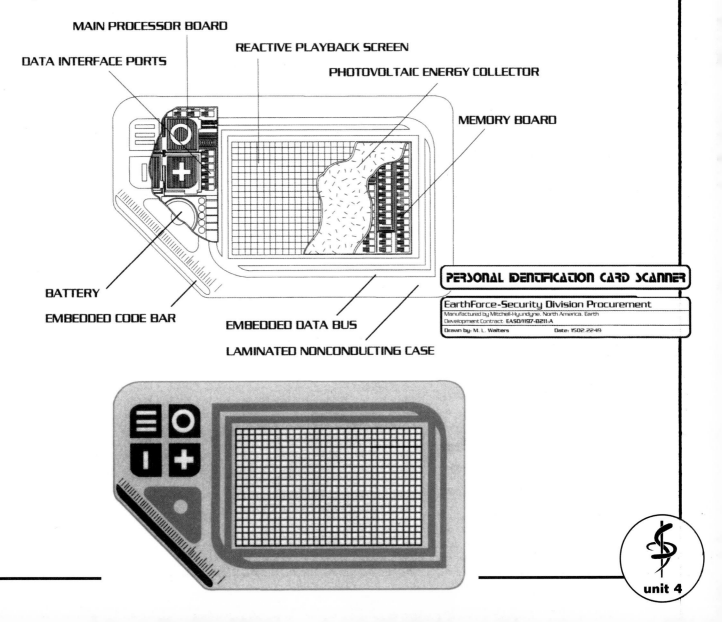

MAIN PROCESSOR BOARD

DATA INTERFACE PORTS

REACTIVE PLAYBACK SCREEN

PHOTOVOLTAIC ENERGY COLLECTOR

MEMORY BOARD

BATTERY

EMBEDDED CODE BAR

EMBEDDED DATA BUS

LAMINATED NONCONDUCTING CASE

PERSONAL IDENTIFICATION CARD SCANNER

EarthForce-Security Division Procurement
Manufactured by Mitchell-Hyundyne, North America, Earth
Development Contract: EASO/1197-8211:A
Drawn by: M. L. Walters   Date: 1502.2249

unit 4

4.6 ACCIDENT & EMERGENCY

A ccident and emergency operations are run jointly by Security and medlab. There are specific firemen on the station, but all Babylon 5 staff members are trained in fire fighting.

Medlab

There are five medlabs total. Medlab 1 was originally located in Blue Sector but was moved to Red Sector at the beginning of 2260.

Whenever possible medlab will treat all ailments for all species. There is a special isolab where patients can be isolated if they are suffering from a contagious disease or require a nonterran atmosphere. Unfortunately, medlab is not a free service and is therefore unavailable Down Below. (Intelligence reports indicate that a free clinic is run for hullrats who cannot afford private medical insurance.)

Usually minimum surgery is done to stabilize the condition of the patients, and then patients are moved to specialized facilities off-station. However, this is not always possible, and the procedure is changing.

The facility is small and can quickly get overrun, as happened during the Markab plague and the influx of Narn refugees from the Narn-Centauri War.

You may be required to be on "watch" duty if there is an important patient in medlab, such as an ambassador.

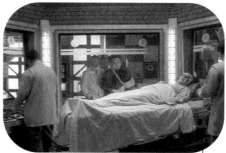

Centauri ambassador Londo Mollari in sickbay

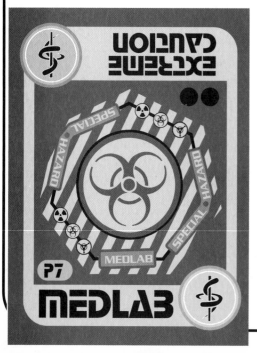

Free Medicine

"Since our secession, finance has been at a premium. Robbing the system of any part of its rightful revenue constitutes a class one offense, since it puts the safety of the station and therefore all our lives at risk. So technically, providing free medical services is a crime. Then again, so's littering Down Below with dead bodies. Anyway. I've never seen a free clinic down there—and neither have you."—MG

As you are now on Babylon 5 you should have had the following vaccinations. If you have not, you MUST visit medlab now:

- Ø Centauri Flu
- Ø Antarean Gonorrhea
- Ø Narn Serum Sickness
- Ø Pak'ma'ra Erysipelas
- Ø Drazi Gastroenteritis
- Ø Minbari Infectious Mononucleosis
- Ø Tuchan Leprosy
- Ø Vree Encephalitis
- Ø Morbis Medacarbolis

Dr. Franklin checks on a patient

Medical emergencies arise as the result of Shadow technology

Under station regulations, any cases of the following must be reported and quarantined:

- Ø Staffords Disease
- Ø Chalmers Syndrome
- Ø Eli'Panzt'runk Nose

Dr. Franklin performs surgery

unit 4

4.7 DISEASE—RISKS & PREVENTION

Food

Various foodstuffs are dangerous to different species. It is worth being conversant with the main sources of nourishment both for your own and for other species.

The Pak'ma'ra, being carrion eaters, never eat at the fast-food outlets. Only alien foods that are known to be safe for Humans are available at the legitimate food outlets (this does not apply to Down Below).

A Centauri banquet

You may find yourself involved in the occasional poisoning incident, but unless stomach pumps are used, it is impossible to find out what tourists have eaten. In some cases it is best not to know.

There are certain foodstuffs common to all races. The Minbari Flarn is acknowledged as being a somewhat boring food. The Narn Pitlok is an animal much like a sheep but with a leathery hide and a horn. Strangely, it moves backward. Pitlok tastes a bit like Antarean Ntchtlaantl steeped in orange juice.

Spoo is also a common food. All races like Spoo, but the Pak'ma'ra publicly denounce it as hateful; however, they are one of the main consumers of Spoo, getting their stock from the black market.

Spoo are of the Nematoda family (imagine a five-meter-long earthworm) and are reviled by most civilized societies without any good reason. Many races acknowledge it as the ugliest creature in the known universe. Spoo are raised on tropical ranches and move very slowly (six inches a year is considered rushing).

Raising Spoo on ranches is not hard work. They require damp, warm conditions and travel in herds. Around two hundred Spoo can be left on their own and will multiply without further assistance. However, working on Spoo farms can induce depression, as the Spoo take their name from the constant sighs emitted from more than seventeen bodily orifices.

When Spoo are harvested, special help lines are set up for those unfortunate enough to hear the sighing as the creatures are culled. Spoo is served in white, pasty cubes that are cooked at 62 degrees. Raw Spoo is considered a delicacy by the Narn but is generally banned from Babylon 5 because unsterilized Spoo contains the poisonous eggs of the adult male. Narn gastrointestinal flora is the only known gastrointestinal flora that can break down and metabolize Spoo eggs.

By an odd coincidence, currently being researched heavily by both the Mathematics Department of the University of Vienna and the Research and Development Department of Fifty-Seven Foods Ltd., all known species of intelligent life have developed a dish that is the equivalent of Swedish meatballs. The Vorlon equivalent is named Elaa and is itself intelligent.

unit 4

Medlab

"The medlab facilities on the station are really good. The doctor saved my life when I contracted Monoid Inflatatitus. The Deep Space Travel Agency's medical insurance even paid for the first 1,900 credits of the treatment."
—Adrian Middleton, Visitor to Babylon 5

Dangerous species

The following creatures are dangerous:

- Ø Na'ka'leen feeder—consumes neurotransmitter chemicals, thus causing mindwipe or death
- Ø A noncorporeal life-form from Sector 14—this creature has the ability to take over the host, inducing behavioral changes through hallucinations and altered emotional states. Both the EA Special Weapons Division and the Society for the Legalization of the Use of Recreational Drugs have issued special edicts to protect this species and obtain samples for research.
- Ø Grylor—a flying creature from Jaros 7 (has a pointed head, teeth, a long tail, and claws on the hind legs and forewings)
- Ø Khaleds—vicious creatures that believe they are superior to all other creatures in the universe
- Ø Vindrizzi—life-forms that wrap themselves around a host's spinal column in order to survive. Their purpose is to catalog history.

A Na'ka'leen feeder

Sheridan about to meet a noncorporeal life-form that could prove dangerous

Ø Pogles—woodland creatures of Idanna 4 that induce emotional changes in their victims through a form of electrical induction similar to that of the eel

Ø Hobbs—small, insectlike creatures that operate as a "hive" entity

Ø Cromags—these creatures have a tendency to kill and eat their victims before vanishing into thin air.

Ø Mothren—creatures that are constantly taking over other bodies as they try to find a new home after their planet was destroyed

Ø Clan Ga'Arhz—metallic, cloth-skinned creatures that inhabit a small moonlet in Area 19. Their intelligence cannot be determined, since their language—a series of dolphinlike whistles—has never been translated. Research conducted in the last hundred years suggests that the Clan Ga'Arhz live in symbiosis with a subterranean—possibly reptilian—life-form that provides them with food in exchange for trivial items and a unique liquid form of metallic-based avian life.

Toilet Facilities

Some toilets can be considered biohazards, and notice must be taken of the signs indicating which races can use the facilities.

There is considerable disease risk, and there are plans to install sensors at the entrances to facilities. An alert will be called in Security if someone enters a toilet that is not designated for his or her race. These persons are to be arrested immediately, as this is a very serious offense.

Centauri, Narn, and Minbari toilets are safe for Humans. However, Narn urinals are positioned horizontally, making it hard for Humans to use them. Minbari toilets have strict ceremonies that are to be followed before one actually uses the facility. The B'y'Zond race has its own facility, as their excrement can achieve a high level of toxicity that has been known to affect the other races on Babylon 5.

Technicians are on around-the-clock standby since it was discovered that an amino acid chain contained in Varteck urine can break down the molecular structure of all types of metallic and ceramic composites. Special diamond splash guards are under development to prevent further incidences of hull breach, such as the one in Red Four in which three Varteck suffered decompression injuries.

unit 4

In this unit we will be looking at the more high-risk situations you may get involved with on Babylon 5, including terrorist action, ambassadorial protection, and riots. Special training will be given in week seventeen of your advanced training course.
In this manual, such incidents will be reviewed on a case-by-case basis.

5.1 TERRORISM

Terrorism comes in many forms, from individuals with grudges to organized groups with political or humanitarian aims. It is not our job to get involved in the politics of any situation. We are there to provide Security. If Spoo farmers are threatened by animal rights activists, it is our duty to protect the Spoo.

Security has the power to detain suspects for two days before charging them. This can be stretched to five days if a member of the command staff agrees, after which the suspects should be charged or released. We also have the power to restrict the movement of terrorist subjects between areas of the station.

Cooperation between governments is essential in the battle against terrorism. This may be problematic for Babylon 5 since the split from Earth, as Earth's actions against us could be considered terrorism.

Free Phobos

Free Phobos was an alleged radical anti–Psi Corps group that in fact turned out to be a front for the Mix to gain control of Psi Corps. This did not work, and the group has not been heard of for some time.

Free Mars

Before Mars's liberation, Free Mars was a radical organization whose goal was the establishment of Mars as a free state, not associated with Earth and not part of the Alliance. Originally a

Unit 5: Special Internal Security Measures

Free Mars

"Yes, I was a member of Free Mars. What did you expect, for us to sit back and play dominoes while our colonies were bombed, our farms wiped out, our families killed? The hell with that. The Senate's got it all wrong. Free Mars will make Earth sit up and listen. Clark doesn't care about the colonies; he's only interested in what essential supplies he can steal from us. He's killing us to make his own people fat. We won't stand for it!"

—Ryan K. Johnson, Spokesman, Free Mars

humanitarian movement seeking independence through political pressure and peaceful protests, Free Mars eventually concluded that its goal could be reached only through violence.

In 2258 the movement led the rebellion against the Earth-appointed government. The movement has been blamed for many things it has not actually been involved in, such as the bombing of Psi Corps by the Arthur Malten radical group. Free Mars conducted terrorist campaigns against military targets to force Earth to withdraw from Mars. They carried out attacks on Earth to further their aim. Babylon 5 was a site of Free Mars activity, but since its secession and the Mars liberation, the station is no longer considered a target.

The "Mad Bomber" Case

Robert Carlsen worked for Babylon 5's Engineering and Station Maintenance Division from January 11, 2260. He was a quiet man, well spoken but possessed of a bad temper in odd moments. Unknown to us, Carlsen had lost his family and previous job in a tragic accident. But instead of getting counseling to help him recover from this tragedy, Carlsen allowed his pain to fester. He stole explosives from the ice-mining operation on Proxima 3 and brought them to Babylon 5 to perpetrate random acts of terrorism. These acts nearly killed the Minbari aide Lennier, while both the Centauri ambassador Londo Mollari and the Narn citizen G'Kar were trapped in a lift. Carlsen then went on to mine the station's fusion core, an act that could have destroyed the station and the lives of everyone on it.

Captain Sheridan eventually discovered his hideout and got the necessary information to stop him from blowing up the station's fusion reactors.

Carlsen was shot dead when a tactical squad stormed his quarters.

unit 5

5.2 AMBASSADORIAL PROTECTION/SECURITY PROCEDURE

The Ambassadorial Ring is to be accessed by ambassadors, their staffs, Security, and invited guests only. The whole ring is secure—we have a highly effective Security cordon that is backed up by cameras and sensors that monitor the area twenty-four hours a day.

The Babylon 5 Advisory Council

The Babylon 5 Advisory Council is made up of the Earth Alliance, Minbari Federation, Centauri Republic, Narn Regime, Vorlon Empire, and League of Non-Aligned Worlds.

The Council functions in the same way as the old U.N. Security Council on Earth. The membership consists of representatives from major governments. Each representative has one vote. If the Council is deadlocked, the League of Non-Aligned Worlds has the deciding vote.

The Advisory Council intervened in the Narn attack on Ragesh 3, the final Centauri attack on the Narn, the framing of Sinclair for the attempted murder of Ambassador Kosh, and the arrival of Deathwalker and was instrumental in maintaining the security of the whole galaxy during the Shadow War.

During sessions, maximum security is in place.

Ambassadorial Duty

"Most days ambassadorial duty is about as interesting as guarding a can of beans. Then again, everyone has his moments. Once the Narn ambassador offered me three hundred credits to look the other way while certain Human women visited his quarters. On the advice of Mr. Garibaldi, I took the bribe and passed the money on to the Prostitutes Legalization and Protection Fund. Minus a ten percent commission, of course."
—Andrew Hornby, Security Officer

Assassination Attempts

With the high number of races on-station at any one time, not forgetting the importance of ambassadors, it is not surprising that there have been assassination attempts. These attempts can come from individuals or from groups and governments. The Ankh are a particular race to watch as they have a meticulous code of death honor. The Narn also have an Assassins' Guild built into their culture in the form of the Thenta Makur.

The Soul Hunter race is feared by many, but they are not assassins. They believe they can capture the soul upon death. A rogue Soul Hunter kidnapped Ambassador Delenn, intending to kill her and capture her soul. Read Dr. Franklin's psychological report for a full profile of the Soul Hunters and other similar races.

The Thenta Makur had a contract on G'Kar.

G'Kar tried to kill Londo Mollari.

A Minbari assassin tried to kill Kosh and frame Commander Sinclair for the murder.

The Homeguard has attempted a number of assassinations, including one on a League ambassador.

The Nightwatch attempted to have Delenn killed.

The Thenta Makur traditionally leave a black flower with their intended victims before striking. Tu'Pari, a member of the Thenta Makur, was commissioned by Councillor Du'Rog to kill Ambassador G'Kar. It is a distinct possibility that other blood oaths are in force.

Job Security

"My dad always said, 'You want a job for life—you can't beat death.'"
—Karen Smallwood, Undertaker

Diplomatic Immunity

Diplomatic immunity is a touchy area, and the rules are quite grey in places, open to interpretation. Diplomatic immunity is offered only to ambassadorial staff members and their aides. In certain situations ambassadors can offer diplomatic protection to civilian individuals. However, in cases like that the government in question must assume full responsibility for the acts of the guest.

Immunity can be the cause of irresponsible behavior. There was a fight in the casino involving Ambassador Mollari and Minbari aide Lennier, neither of whom could be arrested. Lennier voluntarily paid for damages. Mollari tried to sue for damages.

On another occasion Ambassador Mollari offered the protection of his office to Mr. Morden. That act resulted in tension between Ambassador Mollari and Captain Sheridan.

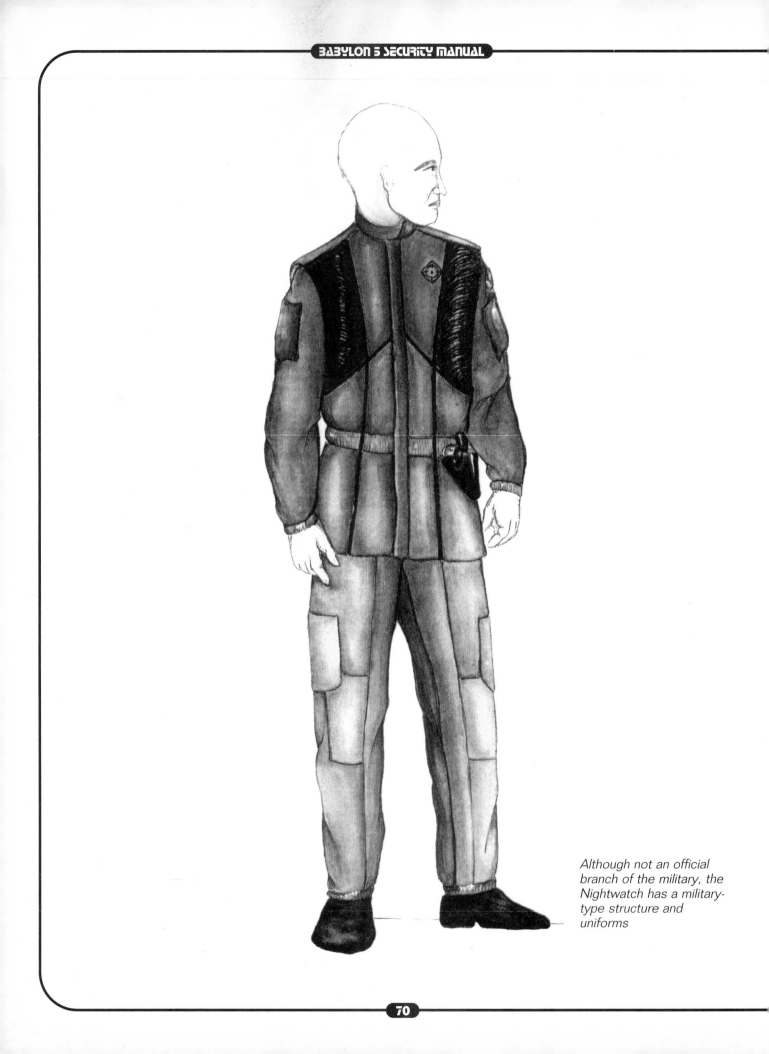

Although not an official branch of the military, the Nightwatch has a military-type structure and uniforms

NIGHTWATCH

Nightwatch

Nightwatch was formed in 2259 and is an organization of informers recruited by the Ministry of Peace. Experience has proved that their actions invoke anything but peace. They have now been banned from the station.

Nightwatch tries to recruit highly placed individuals. Refusal to cooperate is often met with bribery, intense moral and emotional blackmail, or even sexual bribery.

Security Chief Zack Allan joined Nightwatch at the beginning and was rewarded with a payment of fifty credits a month.

Nightwatch

"They told us to be on our guard against the enemy. They told us the enemy was insidious and cunning. They told us the enemy never sleeps. It was ages before I realized they were the enemy—and I was one, too."
—Zack Allan, Former Nightwatch Member

"Yes, I reported staff members of Babylon 5! The place is full of traitors. Earth was our cradle. Earth nurtured us, gave us everything. Nightwatch was just doing its duty to protect Earth. 'It's a matter of historical precedent that we always bite the hand that feeds us.' That has to stop."
—Chris Mayell, Nightwatch Member

Nightwatch was the eyes and ears of President Clark. They reported any anti-Earth opinions or actions and were empowered to act appropriately outside the local chain of command. Ironically, Nightwatch took its name from the time in Earth history when brave citizens stood in the dark watching for enemies, but it later corrupted the ideal into a totalitarian view.

Mr. Welles, a senior member of Nightwatch, would come down hard on anything he considered anti-Earth, citing "misinformation" or "harmful ideas"; for example, he had a shop shut on the Zocalo after the keeper complained about new import regulations. Welles was informed by a Nightwatch member working in C&C that Babylon 5 was sheltering a Narn cruiser. He immediately informed the Centauri. An incident occurred that resulted in massive destruction and loss of life.

Nightwatch was discovered to be working against the command staff of Babylon 5 when former member Zack Allan bravely led it into a trap. Allan was offered the Medal of Outstanding Valor but refused to accept it. For further information, see Unit 8 "Black Operations."

5.3 RIOTS

(See also Unit 2 "Riot Gear.")

There have been a number of incidents on Babylon 5 that can be classified as riots.

A minor incident involved some of the 25,000 ground infantrymen on layover en route to Akdor to stop the civil war there. See the notes on the Dockers' Guild strike and the use of the Rush Act.

A major riot occurred when the Mars attack broke. Another happened when news broke of the Centauri's use of illegal mass drivers during the Narn-Centauri War.

Worse than all of these incidents was the civil unrest after the announcement of the reinstatement of the death penalty by spacing for an individual of the newly contacted Tuchanq species.

Riots usually are controlled by curfew, "lockdown," or morph gas. In rare instances Security Forces are required to use force.

During riots you will be expected to counter the use of various weapons. The weapons will be of both terrestrial and nonterrestrial origin. Your life and the lives of those around you will depend on your knowledge of these weapons. Here is a list of weapons you will need to be familiar with during normal duties.

Hand-to-Hand: Brass knuckles, clubs, EF-issue, nightstick, staff (various), Minbari fighting pike, Katak, bladed weapons (various)

Handguns: W&G Model 10, Auricon EF-7, Kalet Avenger, Tromo handgun, PPG, Sha'ann PP weapon, Coleman .22, Coleman Magnum, U-Teck Stinger Mk II, PPK 7mm (also known as a "slugthrower"; this is a collector's piece)

Longarms: W&G Model 21, Auricon EF-PR, Wesson Sportsman, crossbow, longbow, flamethrower (various)

You also may encounter those trained in a variety of martial arts:

Human: Aikido, karate, kenjitsu (various)
Narn: Then'Sha'Tur
Minbari: Kalan'tha
Centauri: Tronno, Coutari
League Worlds: Venusian aikido, J'Ten Krimbo

Riots

Stuart Vandall: "I stepped off the Grishnaknh *straight into the riot caused by the Earth/Mars attacks. Luckily, my brother was waiting for me and knew there would probably be trouble.*"

Carl Vandall: "It was very worrying. I knew riots had broken out, and so I went to meet my brother. Security was very efficient and helped get us to safety."

unit 5

Unit 6: EXTERNAL DEFENSE

External defense is an important part of Babylon 5 Security. We have been the subject of attacks from alien forces, have been an innocent victim in the Earth "civil war" (which included being boarded by EA troops), and have been caught between warring factions.

The station was also the center of operations during the Shadow War and last year was surrounded by Shadow ships. It is, unfortunately, a fact we have to deal with that these sorts of attacks and threats will probably continue.

6.1 PROCEDURE IN THE EVENT OF INVASION

In the event of any external threat you will be expected to move immediately to your designated area.

Alarms will sound, and civilians should move in an orderly manner to the nearest shelter or stay in their quarters. Starfury squadrons will be scrambled, and blast doors will seal all external ports. Internal blast doors will divide the station into airtight compartments in case of hull breach. Emergency survival kits are located at various points in these sections (check the computer for availability near your area and be aware of them).

Breathing apparatus (including alien atmospheres) will drop from above in cases of breach. However, this is not applicable to some parts of the station.

Spare riot gear should be kept near your battle station and should be worn at times of emergency, as you can expect panic among the civilian population and possible outbreaks of violence and crime.

Heavy weapons are also kept near emergency stations in case of boarding. Most of the squads assigned to counter boarding parties are made up of Narn recruits; however, you

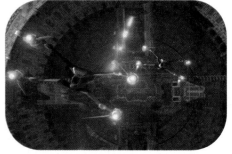
Thunderbolts attacking Babylon 5

Earth Alliance invasion attack fleet

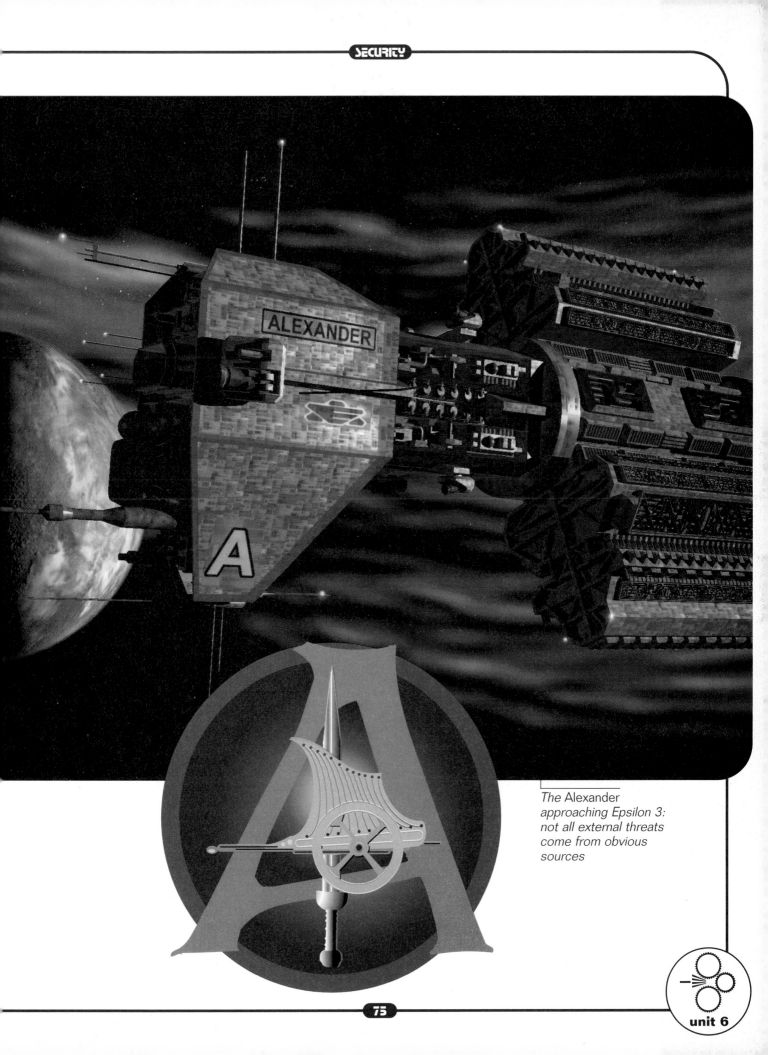

The Alexander *approaching Epsilon 3: not all external threats come from obvious sources*

unit 6

will be expected to join them and defend your station if any battle should reach you.

In emergency situations it is vital to keep communications to a minimum. It is not necessary to report public disturbances, and you will be expected to use your own common sense and judgment. If you do need reinforcements to keep order, you should contact C&C or Security Central.

Obviously, if there is a need for medical attention, contact medlab. Hull breaches are automatically detected and reported to repair crews. If there is a boarding party in your section, you are authorized to draft civilian help and must report to C&C and/or Security Central to obtain backup.

Captain Sheridan's former command, the *Agamemnon*

Hull breaching pods pose major problems

The Agamemnon hunts the White Star near Jupiter

unit 6

External Defenses Overview

As far as external defense goes, there are a number of options. First, we rely heavily on the Starfury squadrons and any Minbari or League ships on patrol at the time. Additional defense includes the weapons grid and the >>CLASSIFIED<< on Epsilon 3.

Space suits are available for external combat and rescue operations. The suits we use are directly descended from ones developed by NASA and also are used in the many docking operations in the cargo bays. These docking operations often require the assistance of workers in EVA (extravehicular activity) suits.

Scanners are located along the outer hull of the station and are used to coordinate defense. Maintenance 'bots are also used to monitor any battle outside and provide a more maneuverable picture. They are all used in tandem with the defense grid.

Minbari fighter

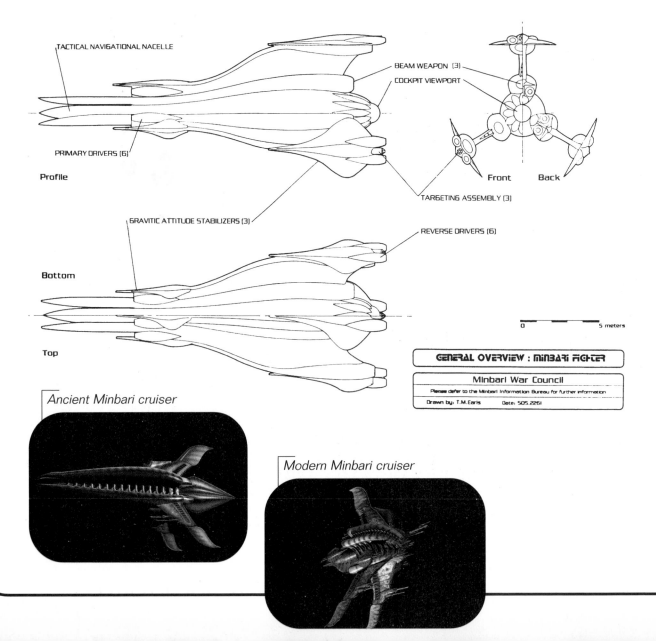

TACTICAL NAVIGATIONAL NACELLE

BEAM WEAPON (3)

COCKPIT VIEWPORT

PRIMARY DRIVERS (6)

Profile

Front   Back

TARGETING ASSEMBLY (3)

GRAVITIC ATTITUDE STABILIZERS (3)

REVERSE DRIVERS (6)

Bottom

Top

0   5 meters

GENERAL OVERVIEW : MINBARI FIGHTER

Minbari War Council

Please defer to the Minbari Information Bureau for further information

Drawn by: T.M.Earls   Date: 505.2261

Ancient Minbari cruiser

Modern Minbari cruiser

Minbari fliers

Vree saucer

The First Ones at Sigma 957

Drazi Sunhawk

Brakiri ship

Narn cruiser

Narn fighter

unit 6

Exterior Equipment

Cambots are used within and outside the ship to monitor possible defense risks and, on extremely rare occasions, by commercial broadcast crews

Maintenance 'bots make external repairs after attacks

Salvage One, *used to remove debris after an attack*

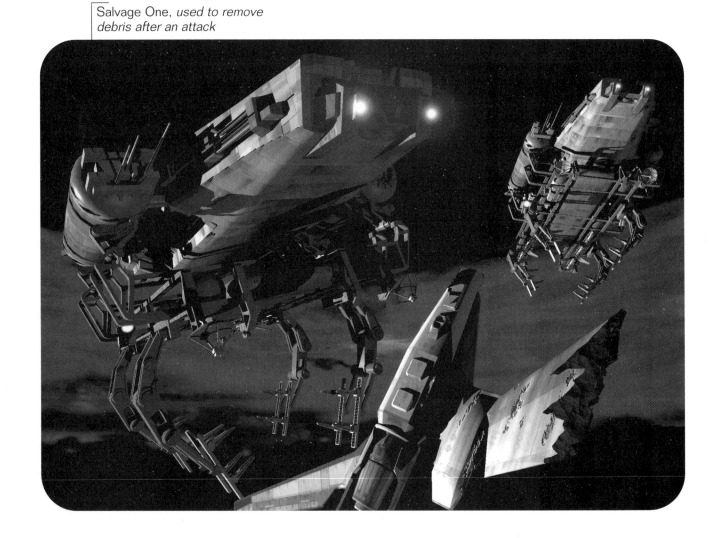

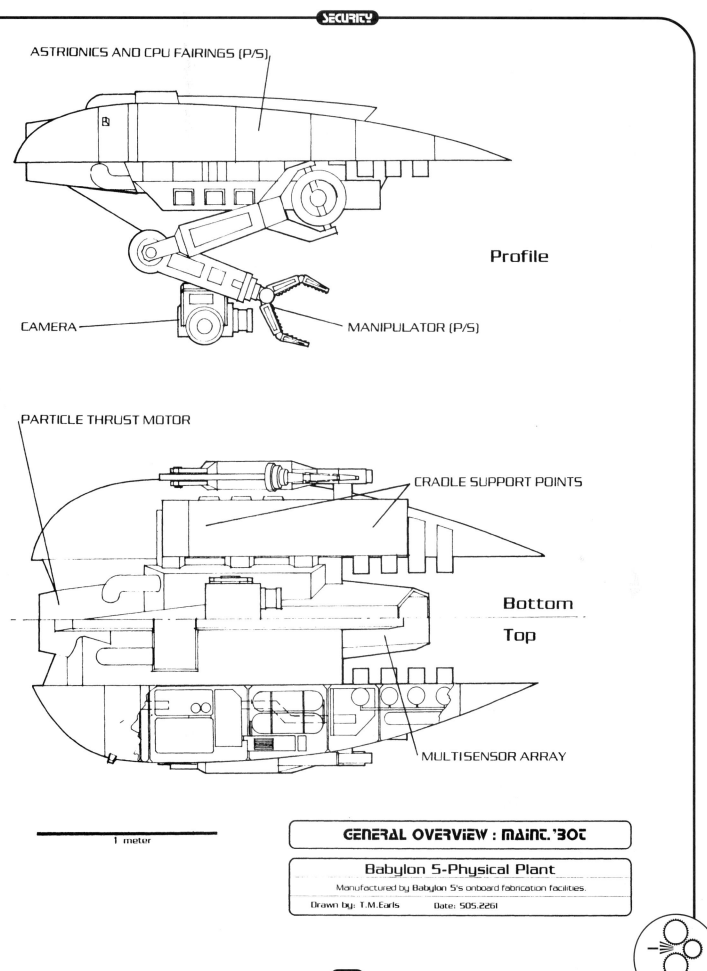

ASTRIONICS AND CPU FAIRINGS (P/S)

Profile

CAMERA

MANIPULATOR (P/S)

PARTICLE THRUST MOTOR

CRADLE SUPPORT POINTS

Bottom

Top

MULTISENSOR ARRAY

1 meter

GENERAL OVERVIEW : MAINT. 'BOT

Babylon 5-Physical Plant

Manufactured by Babylon 5's onboard fabrication facilities.

Drawn by: T.M.Earls   Date: 505.2261

unit 6

6.2 THE STARFURIES

We have two main models of Starfury at our disposal: the SA-23 Mitchell-Hyundyne and the SA-23E.

The SA-23 Mitchell-Hyundyne is a standard EA nonatmospheric fighter with several configurations, while the SA-23E is the standard lightweight version. We have a few that have been modified for atmospheric combat.

We have four launch bays with twenty-seven Starfuries ready to launch at any one time and more on standby launch if needed. As you know, they are single-seat fighters. The operator is both pilot and gunner, so training can be very hard.

They are armed with two forward-firing JC 266 20-megawatt pulse discharge cannons located underneath the cockpit and another two mounted on the top wing above the pilot. These are controlled by a Duffy 1018 MJS smart targeting computer.

There are two types of cannon, with one firing larger, slower but more powerful projectiles while the other fires quick bursts of small projectiles.

Black Omega Starfury

Thunderbolt

Starfury Reliability

"I've been in a number of Starfury squads and have seen plenty of action. The craft are maneuverable and give you a lot of confidence. They're the best we could have. I don't think I'd have survived some of the fights if we'd had any other type of craft.

"As well as the battles and drills, we also have a formation squad that I'm part of. After the recent victory in the Shadow War we provided a display for everyone outside the station, releasing special gas and using certain substances mixed in with the fuel to provide colored trails.

"You might have heard a lot of moonshine about the stuff you see out there. I've heard people say they've seen everything from UFOs to teddy bears. It's all science fiction."
—David McIntee, Starfury Pilot

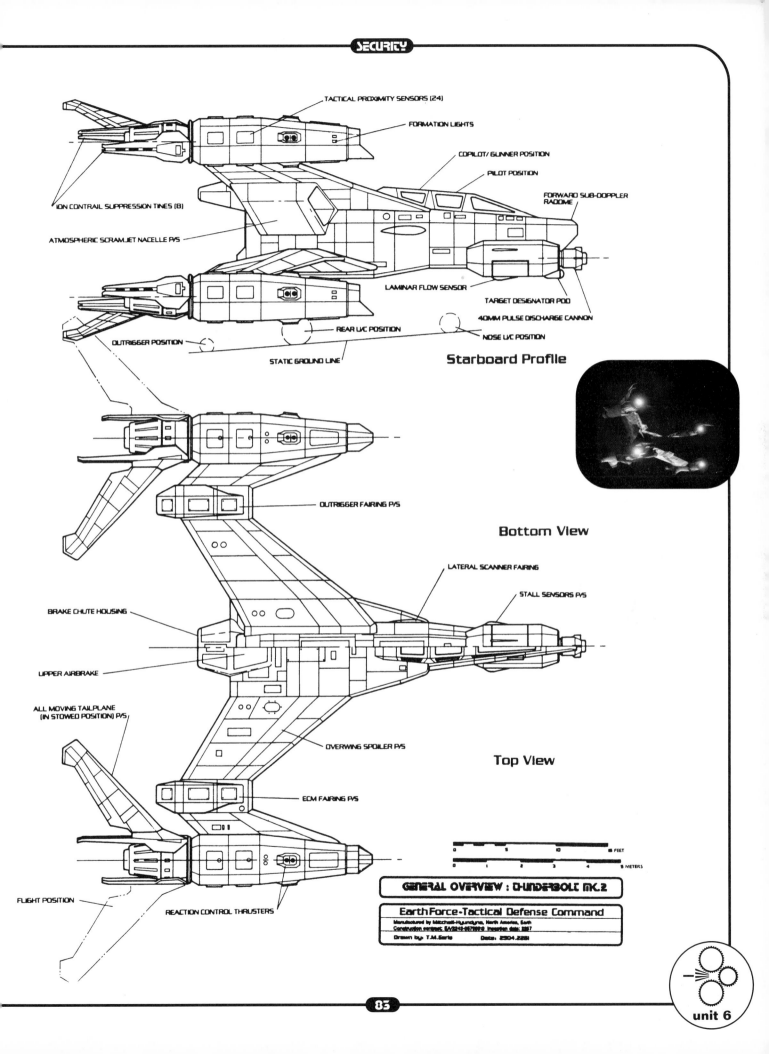

TACTICAL PROXIMITY SENSORS (24)

FORMATION LIGHTS

COPILOT/ GUNNER POSITION

PILOT POSITION

FORWARD SUB-DOPPLER RADOME

ION CONTRAIL SUPPRESSION TINES (8)

ATMOSPHERIC SCRAMJET NACELLE P/S

LAMINAR FLOW SENSOR

TARGET DESIGNATOR POD

40MM PULSE DISCHARGE CANNON

REAR U/C POSITION

NOSE U/C POSITION

OUTRIGGER POSITION

STATIC GROUND LINE

Starboard Profile

OUTRIGGER FAIRING P/S

Bottom View

LATERAL SCANNER FAIRING

STALL SENSORS P/S

BRAKE CHUTE HOUSING

UPPER AIRBRAKE

ALL MOVING TAILPLANE
(IN STOWED POSITION) P/S

OVERWING SPOILER P/S

Top View

ECM FAIRING P/S

FLIGHT POSITION

REACTION CONTROL THRUSTERS

FEET

METERS

GENERAL OVERVIEW : THUNDERBOLT MK.2
Earth Force - Tactical Defense Command
Manufactured by Mitchell-Hyundyne, North America, Earth
Construction contract: EA/9243-067982-2 Insertion date: 1987
Drawn by: T.M.Earle   Date: 2304.2281

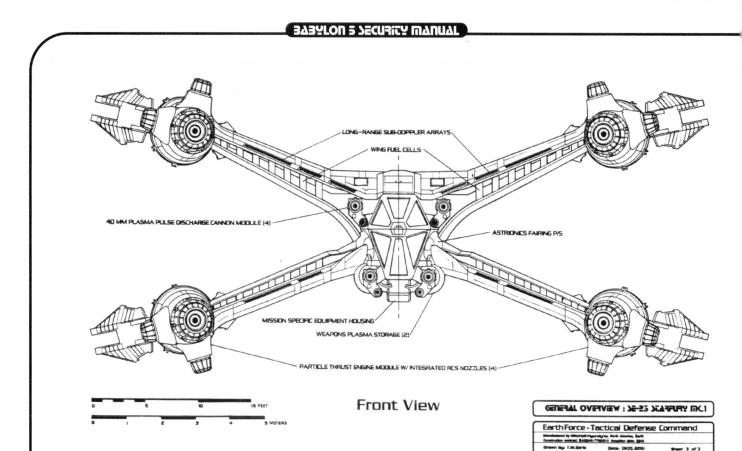

LONG-RANGE SUB-DOPPLER ARRAYS

WING FUEL CELLS

40 MM PLASMA PULSE DISCHARGE CANNON MODULE (4)

ASTRONICS FAIRING P/S

MISSION SPECIFIC EQUIPMENT HOUSING

WEAPONS PLASMA STORAGE (2)

PARTICLE THRUST ENGINE MODULE W/ INTEGRATED RCS NOZZLES (4)

Front View

0   5   10   15 FEET

0   1   2   3   4   5 METERS

GENERAL OVERVIEW : SE-23 STARFURY MK.1
Earth Force - Tactical Defense Command

The newer models are more heavily armed but have various technical problems that must be overcome before they can be brought into full service. There are also atmospheric two-seater models (a heavier military version with turrets fore and aft with heavier shielding and armaments) and one with a tail section and a different type of cockpit.

The distinctive X shape of the fighter is designed to have the thrust (a maximum of 1 km per second) moved away from the ship's center of gravity. The ship's fuel is stored in the wings.

The four Copeland ion engines situated on the edge of the X-foils provide a lot of maneuverability and have directional fins at the rear with thrusters for pitch and yaw control. There are a further four engines on each Starfury that run on vaporized solid propellant. Thanks to its surfeit of engines and thruster power, the Starfury can spin 180 degrees in under a second. It can therefore perform lateral, vertical, and complex roll maneuvers "on a dime."

Each Starfury also has a grappling hook on its ventral surface. The cockpit does not have extensive life support systems, and the pilots wear space suits to survive extreme g-forces and hull breach. There are compensators in the seat structures to allow for rotational and lateral g-forces.

Instruments are located below the main forward cockpit window. Heads-up displays can link to the helmet projectors via an umbilical cable, offering tactical displays superimposed on forward vision. Instrument range varies with local EM conditions. Maximum scope is 70,000 km.

If the vessel is severely damaged, the cockpit is capable of jettisoning away from the main part of the ship.

Thunderbolt

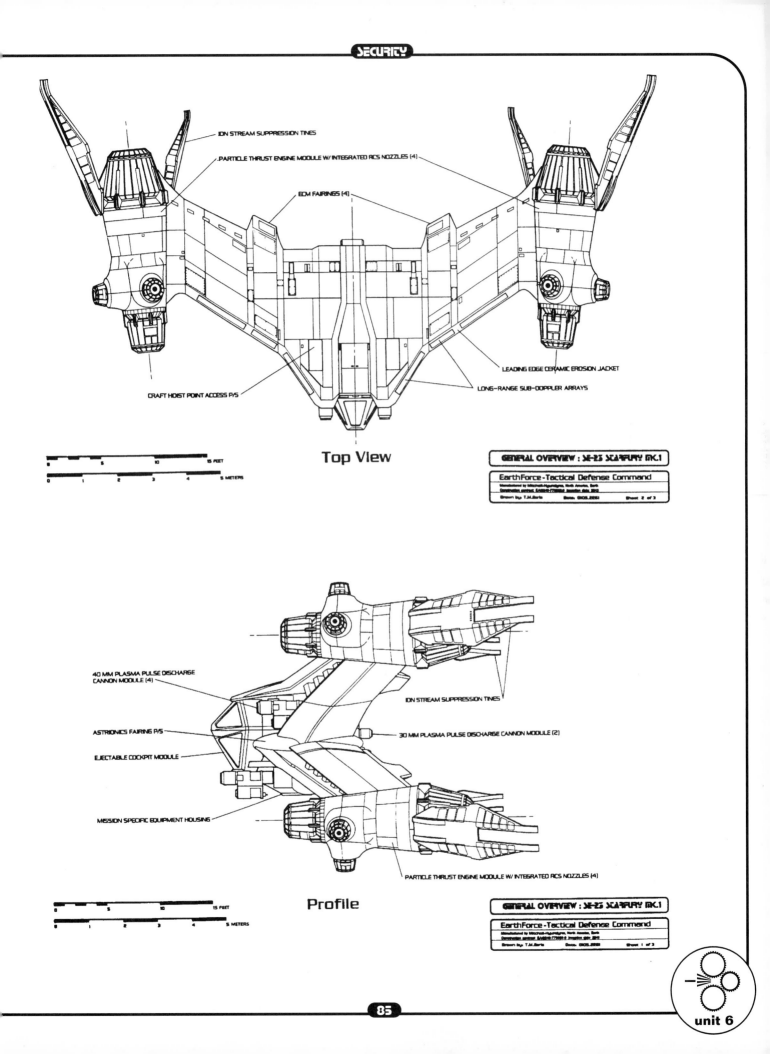

ION STREAM SUPPRESSION TINES

PARTICLE THRUST ENGINE MODULE W/ INTEGRATED RCS NOZZLES (4)

ECM FAIRINGS (4)

CRAFT HOIST POINT ACCESS P/S

LEADING EDGE CERAMIC EROSION JACKET

LONG-RANGE SUB-DOPPLER ARRAYS

Top View

15 FEET

5 METERS

GENERAL OVERVIEW : SE-23 SCARFURY MK.1

EarthForce - Tactical Defense Command

Manufactured by Mitchell-Hyundyne, North America, Earth
Construction contract EA6849-778889 inception date 2242
Drawn by: T.M.Earle   Date: 0305.2261   Sheet 2 of 3

40 MM PLASMA PULSE DISCHARGE
CANNON MODULE (4)

ASTRIONICS FAIRING P/S

EJECTABLE COCKPIT MODULE

MISSION SPECIFIC EQUIPMENT HOUSING

ION STREAM SUPPRESSION TINES

30 MM PLASMA PULSE DISCHARGE CANNON MODULE (2)

PARTICLE THRUST ENGINE MODULE W/ INTEGRATED RCS NOZZLES (4)

Profile

15 FEET

5 METERS

GENERAL OVERVIEW : SE-23 SCARFURY MK.1

EarthForce - Tactical Defense Command

Manufactured by Mitchell-Hyundyne, North America, Earth
Construction contract EA6849-778889 inception date 2242
Drawn by: T.M.Earle   Date: 0305.2261   Sheet 1 of 3

unit 6

Starfury Squadrons

Although not one of Babylon 5's squadrons, Death's Hands—the 361st Tactical Fighter Squadron—probably will be mentioned at some point. This was Commander Sinclair's squadron during the Battle of the Line. You will see pictures of it and other squads from the battle in Starfury crew rooms, etc.

The 361st had a triangular patch with "Starfury" in silver on the back on the upper left angle and FA-23E in the right upper angle with the burner part of the triangle divided in two by a vertical silver stripe, blue on the left and gold on the right. Over this was the design of one of the fighters in full acceleration, leaving trails behind it, and the squadron number and motto "Ugly but well hung" beneath it.

There are many squadrons on Babylon 5. Here are the main ones.

Flying Nightmares, B5FA-1013—Alpha Wing

Members wear a circular patch with the unit's name and number on the outer ring with a Babylon 5 symbol on the left side outlined by vertical red stripes. On the right is a black vertical stripe bordered by "2256."

*Starfuries
hunting Raiders*

Ghost Riders, B5FD-1017—Delta Wing

The unit's name and number are on the outer wing. The Babylon 5 symbol is on the left side outlined in grey stripes, and on the right is a gold vertical stripe bordered by "2257."

Rolling Thunder, B5FB-1014—Beta Wing

The unit's name and number are on the outer wing. The Babylon 5 symbol is on the left side outlined in yellow stripes, and on the right is a silver vertical stripe bordered by "2257."

Air Cavalry, B5F2-1015—Zeta Wing

The unit's name and number are again on the outer wing. The Babylon 5 symbol is on the left side outlined in green stripes, and on the right is a bronze vertical stripe bordered by "2257."

Individual Starfuries

Customized markings are allowed on Starfury wings as long as they are not derogatory to the EA.

- Ⓞ Ivanova's has a two-headed eagle in a stylized form.
- Ⓞ Sheridan's has a flying tiger emblem.
- Ⓞ Sinclair's had chevrons.
- Ⓞ The *Sea Witch* has a blue and green painting of a mermaid.

6.3 DEFENSE GRID

Epsilon 3

The defense grid on the station was upgraded in 2259. It can be used to destroy or disable attacking ships and deflect debris approaching the station.

We have laser cannons, guns, interceptors, and pulse cannons. These and the sophisticated tracking systems have enabled the station to defend itself against warships in the past.

Although we have not called on its help yet in external defense matters, we should also be able to call on the use of the >>CLASSIFIED<< the surface of Epsilon 3. Its >>CLASSIFIED<< is more than sufficient to destroy an entire >>CLASSIFIED<<.

NOTE: Epsilon 3 had a moon before >>CLASSIFIED<<.

>>CLASSIFIED<< in action

unit 6

In this unit we will take a look at the different sectors and power blocks you will be expected to be conversant with (all worlds and colonies are not therefore listed—just the major ones). We will take a look at relevant jumpgates, colonies, etc. More information is available on the computer.

7.1 OVERVIEW

Earth Colonies

Earth Alliance includes fourteen stars and twenty-four planetary bodies.

In the Sol (home) system there are the following worlds and colonies:

- Ø Sol 3 .... Earth
- Ø Sol 3a .... Moon
- Ø Sol 4 .... Mars
- Ø Sol 4a .... Phobos Station
- Ø Sol 4L2 .... Near Mars
- Ø Sol 5 .... Jupiter
- Ø Sol 5a .... Io solar transport and mining colony
- Ø Sol 5b .... Europa
- Ø Sol 5c .... Ganymede

On Betelgeuse there are the Orion 3 and 4 mining worlds. In the Alpha Centauri sector Earth has Proxima and Proxima 3. In Eridanis there is Amador, Pepinia, and Balus, while in the Alpha Lyra sector there is the Vega outpost/colony and the Vega 8 ice mines.

The Aldebaran system has one Earth colony, New Jerusalem, and so do Cyrius and Cyrius 3. Epsilon 3, Euphrates, and Janos 8 are in the same sector as Babylon 5, Epsilon Eridanii 3.

Minbari

The three main worlds besides Minbar are Reticulum, Dorado, and Pictor.

Centauri

The Centauri have three main worlds besides Centauri Prime and Centaurus: Lupis, Crive, and Musca.

Narn

The Narn lost all their worlds and colonies to the Centauri in the recent war but have regained their homeworld and Chameleon (also known as Volans).

Vorlon

The Vorlon sector is located throughout Virgo and Leo with outer worlds that were previously Vorlon colonies, including Hydra, Crater, and Conus. These worlds have, with the end of the Shadow War, been abandoned by the Vorlons and are only now being explored.

Shadows

As with the Vorlons, these worlds have been abandoned and are only now being explored. They go through the Gemini, Cancer, and Taurus sectors near the Rim. There is not yet a full catalogue of Shadow holdings.

Sectors

1 Tigris Sector—neutral space.

4 Earth.

5 Proxima System, including Proxima 3.

7 Specific location is near Babylon 5, 10 degrees counterclockwise to Babylon 5's axis.

10 Specific location is near Babylon 5, 30 degrees counterclockwise to Babylon 5's axis.

14 Three hours travel from Babylon 5 via normal space. This was the region where Babylons 1–4 were built and the site of a spatial rift with extensive tachyon interference. Travel is restricted in this area.

16 Abbai 4.

19 A sector over which negotiations have taken place between the Narn and the Centauri.

21 Akdor—third planet of the Sh'lasson Triumvirate, where a civil war was quashed with help from Earth.

23 Site of the disappearance of the Markab ship *Kartel*, last reported in grid 230 × 9 × 40—this has become legendary.

24/59/58/64 All invaded and devastated by the Dilgar.

29 Site of a Narn colony attacked by the Centauri in the war.

42 Home of the D'Adams.

45 Markab homeworld.

47 Site of Comac 4, a planet destroyed by Jha'dur.

49 Tirolus, destroyed by Jha'dur.

50 Antares Sector—home of the Antareans.

56 Damodocles Sector.

71 Tirolus.

79 Notsalrad.

92 Sector where Streib activity is known to take place. A number of ships were captured by them here.

112 A trade route through this sector has been agreed on between the Minbari and the Centauri.

120 Minbar.

127 Site of an abandoned Centauri colony (they were driven out by the Narn).

128 Garesh 7, a heavily fortified Centauri world.

150 Centauri Prime (seventy-five light-years from Babylon 5).

156 Ragesh 3, former Centauri Agro Colony currently being rebuilt.

157 Quadrant 37, neutral territory between the Narn and the Centauri.

158 Quadrant 14, including the previous Narn colonies on the border of Centauri space.

160 Narn homeworld.

162 Hy'ch 7, Narn colony destroyed by the Dilgar.

175 Sector 70 × 12 × 5 was the site of the deciding battle between allied forces, the Vorlons, and the Shadows at Coriana 6 (which has six billion inhabitants).

202 The Shadows had a base here on Dorak 7.

250 Former site of Z'ha'dum before it was destroyed. The Shadows operated from here.

300 Ikaara 7.

305 Sigma 937. This is a planet in the Narn disputed sector of space where there were signs of significant amounts of Duridium. It was left undeveloped due to strange occurrences at the time, which were later found to have been caused by a race of First Ones.

364 Lordec 4, a colony wiped out by J'hadur.

401 Omeloi—Caliban Sector.

452 Orion—member of EA.

498 Colonies in this sector were among the first to be attacked by the Vorlons. They include Mokafa Station, Drazi Fendamir Research Colony, Kazomi 7, D'Grn 4, G'Gn'Daort, Nacambad Colony, 7 Lukantha, Oqmritkz, Velatasta, Lesser Krindar, and Greater Krindar. Tizino Prime and Dura 7 were destroyed. A great aid effort is currently concentrated in this region.

550 Former Vorlon homeworld.

654 Vega Sector—home of the Vega colonies.

801 Zagros 7—Drazi colony on the edge of Centauri space.

857 Sightings of Shadow vessels took place in this sector before the war.

858 Ventari 3, destroyed by the Vorlons. Jumpgate also destroyed, currently undergoing repairs.

889 Zestus.

900 An area recently mapped in a two-year expedition by the *Cortez.* It is the edge of Vorlon space. A colony here was one of the first to be destroyed by the Shadows.

915 Site of one of the first Shadow attacks (on EAS Eratosthenes).

1025 One of the nearest sectors to the Rim, the border of known space.

Sector 14

See above. This is being flagged, as it is strictly forbidden to all traffic. An unknown entity (a noncorporeal being) came from here, taking over host bodies in order to try to get home.

Jumpgates/Vortex Generators

Jumpgates are the principal means of interstellar travel. A jumpgate is created by a Vortex Generator—a large device that forms an entrance to or an exit from hyperspace so that ships that do not have their own jump point generators can travel through it.

It is a major expenditure of energy to punch in or out of hyperspace; only a few ships have their own generators, and these ships can open small gates only two or three times in a twenty-four-hour period. There is a massive energy requirement which needs jump engines.

The stationary jumpgates have four 10-km-long rods and a stationary generator. There are six sections to each rod, divided equally between six solar panel sections that light up in order to fire into the center, opening a rift in hyperspace.

The rails and charges along the rods are designed to facilitate travel and make the transition to and from hyperspace easier and less abrupt than a ship-mounted transition. The rods are designed to separate from one another and can move to accommodate different size vessels.

Jumpgates cannot be shut down or started up easily. The level of energy needed to maintain one is high. They are usually under the control of a base, and ships are needed to travel to new sectors that do not have them so that new gates can be built.

The crew of a ship must transmit a specific frequency identification to trigger the gate and open a way through. Gates can be programmed to accept only certain frequencies to stop enemies from using them.

Some gates have two parallel constructs, each 1 km long, around 5 km farther out. These structures produce dampening fields to help ships decelerate as they come out of hyperspace.

Jumpgates

"Jumpgate technology was bartered for with the Centauri when our two races first met. Their original asking price was the continent of Africa (for a colony). EarthGov cleverly beat them down to Australia. After meeting the Narn, we realized the Centauri had lied to us. They were so embarrassed, we got Australia back and the jumpgate technology for free."—MG

Earth Alliance cruiser-type starship Hyperion

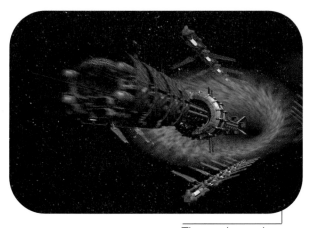

The explorer-class EarthForce ship Cortez

unit 7

Jumpgates act as locator beacons in hyperspace and provide a 3D homing signal that is detectable for 91,000 km. If a gate can respond to a ship's data requests, it can send through data and traffic information.

There is some variation between gates built by different races; for instance, Narn gates have three rods. Mostly, the entry color of the vortex is yellow and the exit is blue.

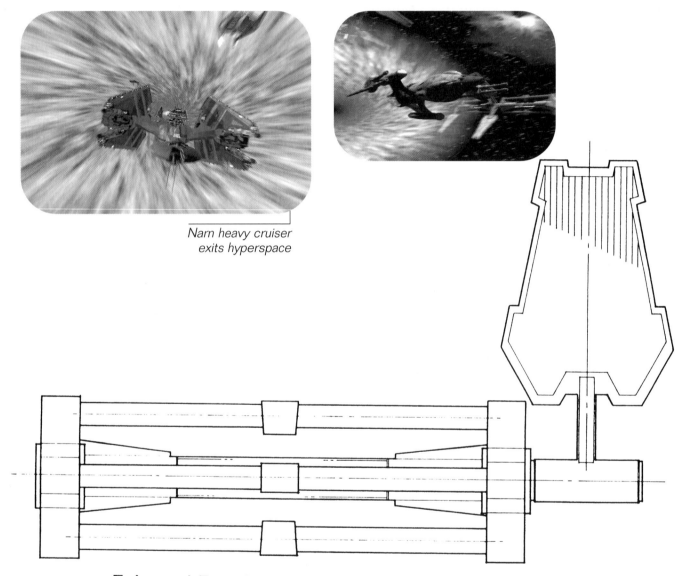

Narn heavy cruiser
exits hyperspace

Enlarged Detail of Typ. Module Assembly

GENERAL OVERVIEW : JUMPGATE

EarthForces-Corps of Engineers

Please defer to the Earth Alliance Ministry of Information for further information

Drawn by: T.M.Earls   Date: 505.2261

SPATIAL CONSTRICTION ARRAY [48]

FIELD PHASING MODULE [28]

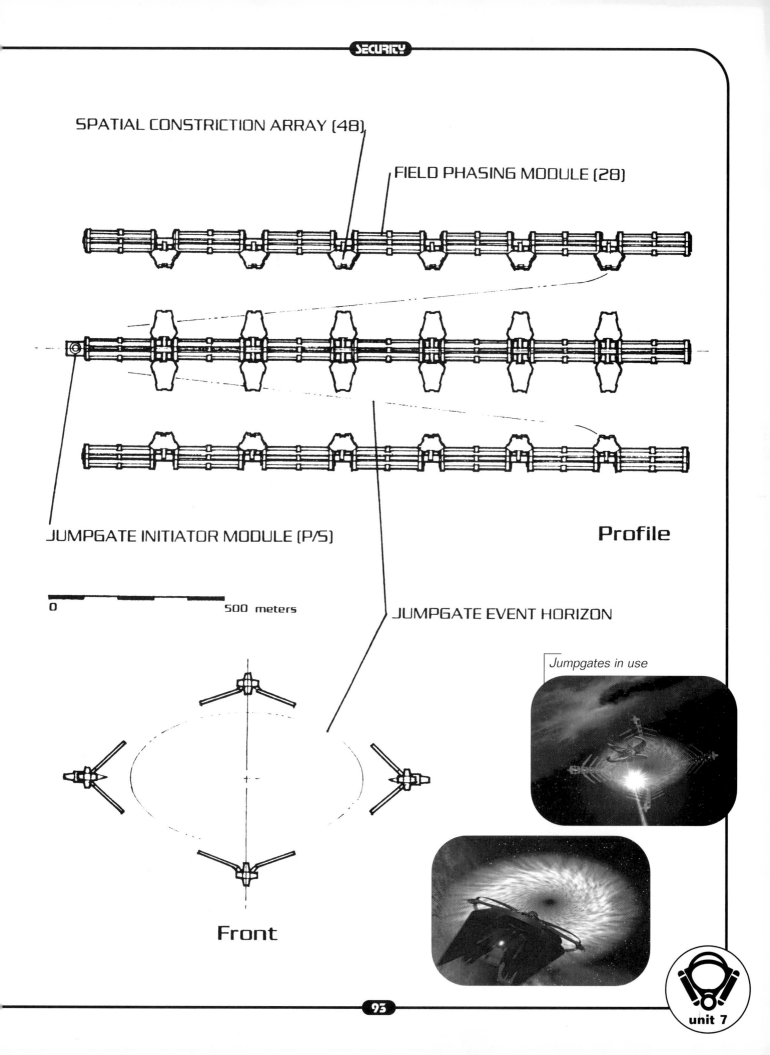

JUMPGATE INITIATOR MODULE [P/S]

Profile

0   500 meters

JUMPGATE EVENT HORIZON

Jumpgates in use

Front

unit 7

7.2 EARTH ALLIANCE AND EARTHFORCE

*E*A's military divisions have different branches, each with a different color uniform. Command staff members wear a traditional blue, Marines olive/brown, and Security grey. These are the only constants.

Ever since the Earth-Minbari War, the Earth authorities have wanted new technology, and there are many research stations set up with ships on constant exploratory missions.

EarthForce fleet in civil war around Jupiter

EA is a political organization based on Earth with numerous regional consortiums—including twenty-four worlds and fourteen star systems—under its jurisdiction. It is structured along the lines of a commonwealth or federation.

It has a single, monolithic voice with regard to foreign policy, interstellar travel, and warfare, with all the appropriate social and legal policies of any government to draw upon.

Individual states, depending on the country or colony, may maintain some semblance of independence and are allowed to make their own rules.

There are still conflicts between Earth countries and colonies. Several countries have recently pulled out of the Earth Alliance in protest, on the grounds that since they do not benefit equally from the exploitation of space, they should not be expected or required to help pay for its development on an equal footing.

SEAL OF THE EARTH ALLIANCE

EarthForce 1

GROPOS in action

There is a president and a Senate consisting of elected representatives from each nation-state, colony, and regional consortium. The number of seats is determined by power and population divisions within states. There are interstellar colonies and "fringe" areas that consider themselves independent.

The EA government is made up of both civilian and military branches. The civilian branch oversees the military, and the Senate oversees EarthForce (the equivalent of an armed services committee).

There are two main branches of EarthForce (fleet and ground forces). Both branches are under the command of the president and are supervised by the Senate Committee for Planetary Security.

The Copernicus

EA consists in the main of Humans, and aliens generally are not integrated into the system except in low-level staffing. However, Earth has made exceptions with a number of cooperative projects with other worlds, such as in the Balus, Orion, Proxima, and Vegan outposts.

Colonial governments do have alien members, but these members are virtual "puppets." This overlap is where EA draws its non-Human members, and only a few worlds have chosen to ally themselves directly with EA. EA may be large but is not on a par with the Centauri Republic.

The IPX science vessel Icarus *en route to Za'ha'dum*

unit 7

7.5 MINBARI FEDERATION

The Minbari Federation is a political organization of Minbari people. The governing body is known as the Grey Council, an organization originally made up of three members from each of the three Minbari castes: warrior, religious, and worker. The Council was disbanded just before the Shadow War and was later reestablished by Delenn after hostilities broke out between the warrior and religious castes. The new Council was formed to give the workers the majority vote, as they represent the majority of the Minbari people.

The Minbari ambassador, Delenn, was a member of the Grey Council and served under one of its famous leaders, Dukhat, before his death in 2245. Delenn was offered the position of leader but declined.

The capital of Minbar is Yedor. Minbar is the seventh planet from its sun. A quarter of its surface is covered by its northern ice cap. It has heavy crystalline deposits. Some Minbari cities are cut directly into these crystalline formations.

Ambassador Delenn

Three members of the Grey Council

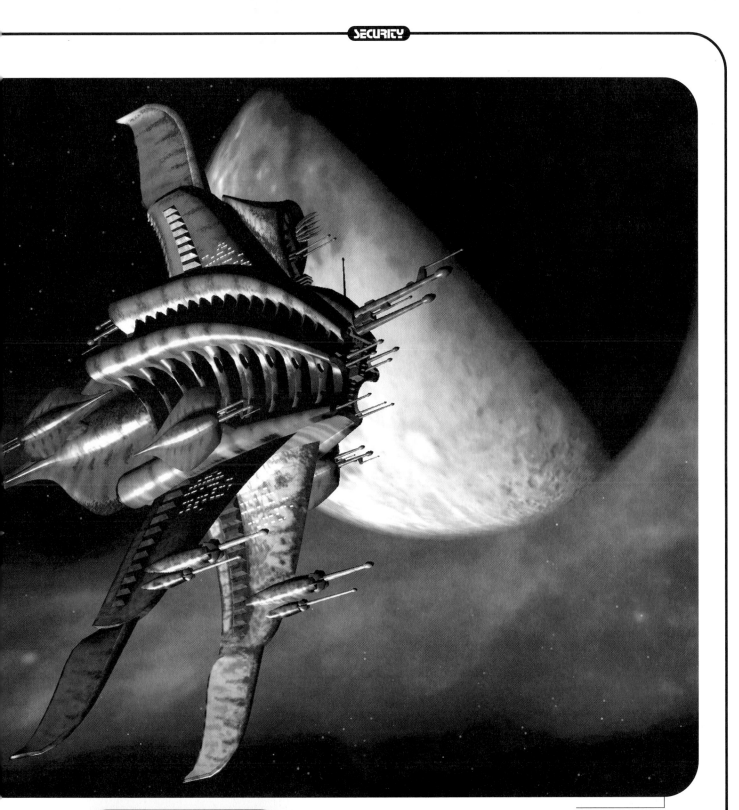

THE TRAGATI
Rogue Minbari cruiser

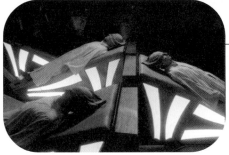

*Minbari telepaths
fighting Shadow ships*

unit 7

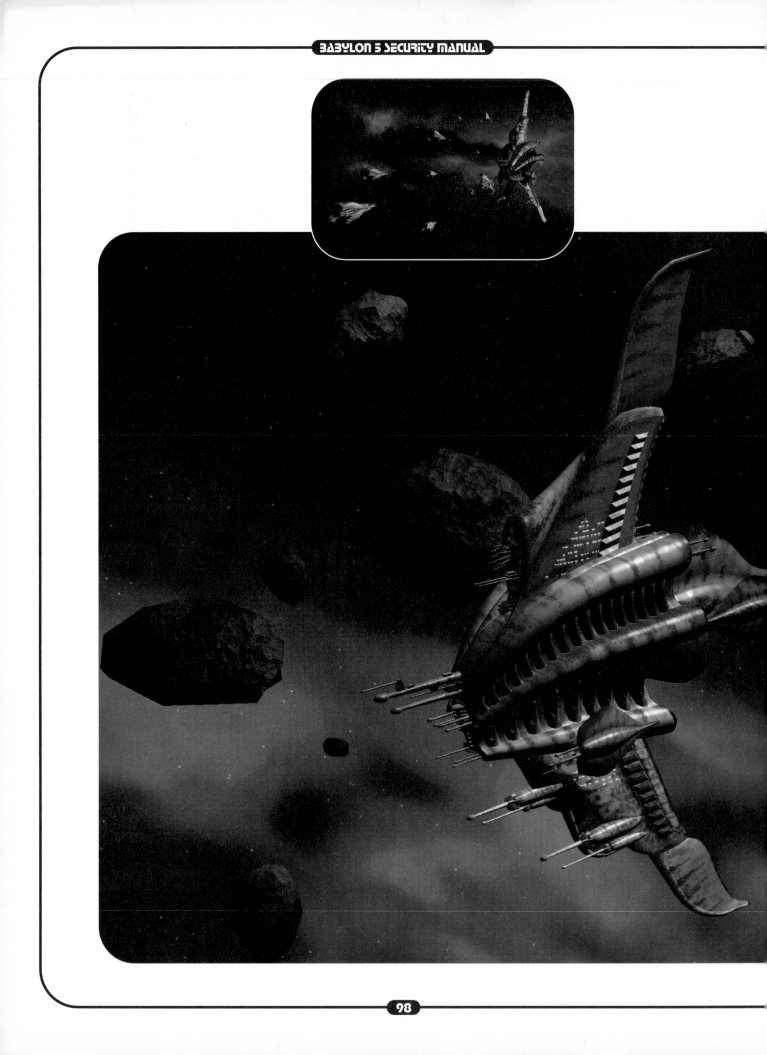

Minbari cruisers
protecting Babylon 5

Views on Minbar

"When I first stepped out onto Minbar, it was like a dream. The crystal structures shone in the light, casting every color imaginable across the landscape. The sight is truly amazing and hard to describe. The Minbari are a peaceful people at heart, and the welcome from the religious caste was very warming."
—Anne Russell,
Ranger Aide to Sinclair

The Crystal City
on Minbar

unit 7

7.4 CENTAURI REPUBLIC

The Centauri Republic is one of the five major governments in known space; it is governed by an emperor. However, after the last emperor died, a prince regent was appointed until a new emperor could be chosen. Londo Mollari currently serves as Prime Minister to the Centauri Republic.

The republic was once very powerful and controlled most of inhabited space. It is now in decline and consists of twelve star systems and tourist attractions such as Davo and Ragesh 3. Its Senate-like body is called the Centaurum.

Centauri Prime was once inhabited by two sentient races, the second known as the Xon. The Xon no longer exist. Details are scarce.

Imperial palace on Centauri Prime

Centauri cruisers

Centauri fighters

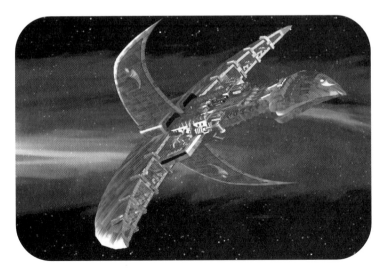

unit 7

7.5 NARN REGIME

The Narn had a political organization characterized by circles of power. These circles were titled the Kha'Ri. In 2260 the Centauri conquered Narn for a second time, killing all but one of the Kha'Ri members and replacing it with a provisional government under their control.

After G'Kar became instrumental in freeing the Narn homeworld from Centauri rule, he was offered the chance to become "Emperor," which he declined. It is not known what sort of organization will form the government of the devastated Narn people.

Narn crime—drug abuse and mind rape

The Narn homeworld

The Narn ceremony of G'Quan Eth'

Narn military outpost at Quadrant 37

Ragesh 3, a Centauri installation attacked by the Narn Regime

Narn cruiser under attack

Narn colony and listening post at Quadrant 14

Detail from a Narn recruiting poster

unit 7

7.6 VORLON EMPIRE

The Vorlon Empire was a political organization of the Vorlons. The Vorlons controlled a vast area of space and avoided all contact with other races until recently.

Scout ships that entered Vorlon space vanished or met with unfortunate accidents. Until these sectors have been explored more fully, a ban on civilian traffic is in force. Until recently the Vorlons had not made war with any races known to us.

The Vorlons are one of the last of the First Ones and first traveled the galaxy a billion years ago. They have been fighting the Shadows in a cold war for the last million years. Vorlon space is around eight days away from Babylon 5.

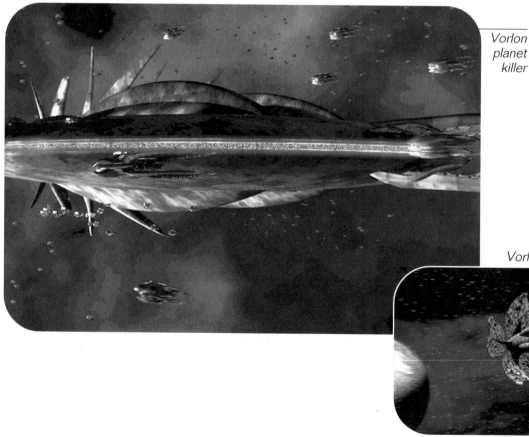

Vorlon planet killer

Vorlon light cruiser

Vorlon fleet

Vorlon decelerating

Vorlon accelerating

unit 7

7.7 NON-ALIGNED WORLDS

The various planets that form the League of Non-Aligned Worlds are mainly located near Centauri space and took the main brunt of their attacks along with those from the Shadows and Vorlons.

They now provide a defensive fleet for Babylon 5 and were instrumental in turning the tide in the Shadow War.

Most recently the member worlds of the League joined the Centauri, Minbari, and Narn in the formation of a new alliance. They named Captain Sheridan president of this new alliance in light of his resignation from EarthForce after the liberation of Earth in 2261.

Vree fleet

Drazi Sunhawk

Pak'ma'ra

Alien pilot

League of Non-Aligned
Worlds: the Llort

unit 7

7.8 RAIDERS

Raiders are space pirates who prey on merchant vessels or passenger liners. One group of Raiders near the station gave us quite a bit of trouble when we went on-line. One faction was supplied by the Narn, while another was supported by the Centauri. There has not been any Raider trouble around Babylon 5 since before the Shadow War.

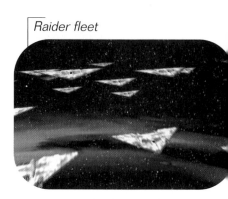
Raider fleet

Raider triangle ship

Raider battlewagon

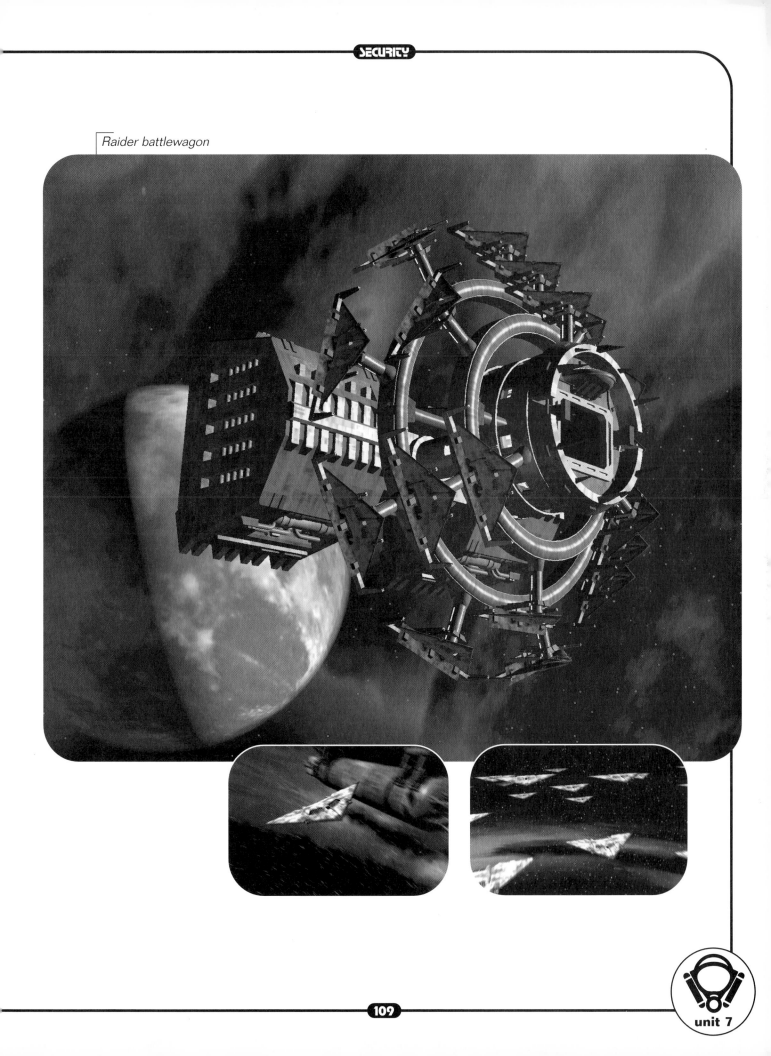

7.9 SHADOWS

The Shadows are an ancient race that almost conquered "known space" a thousand years ago before being pushed back to their homeworld of Z'ha'dum. They are among the First Ones and left for the Rim with the Vorlons.

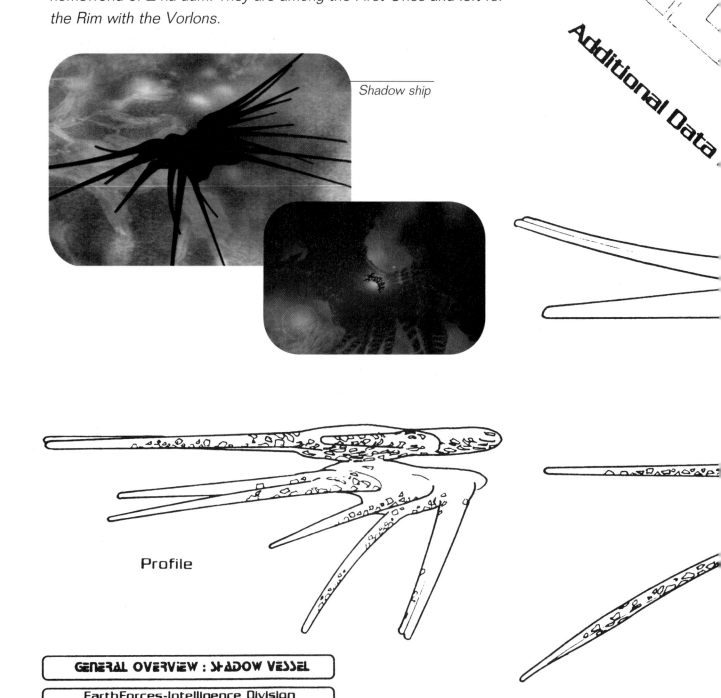

Shadow ship

Additional Data

Profile

GENERAL OVERVIEW : SHADOW VESSEL

EarthForces-Intelligence Division

All other information CLASSIFIED

Drawn by: T.M.Earls   Date: 2604.2261

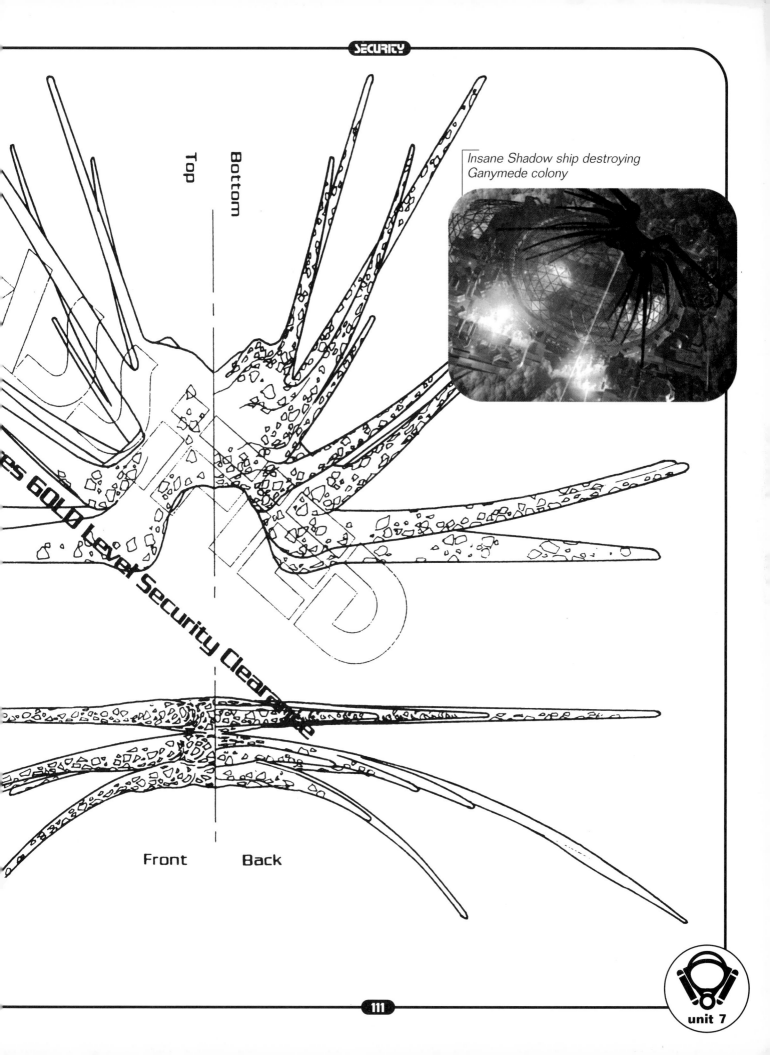

Top

Bottom

es GOLD Level Security Clear...

Insane Shadow ship destroying Ganymede colony

Front   Back

unit 7

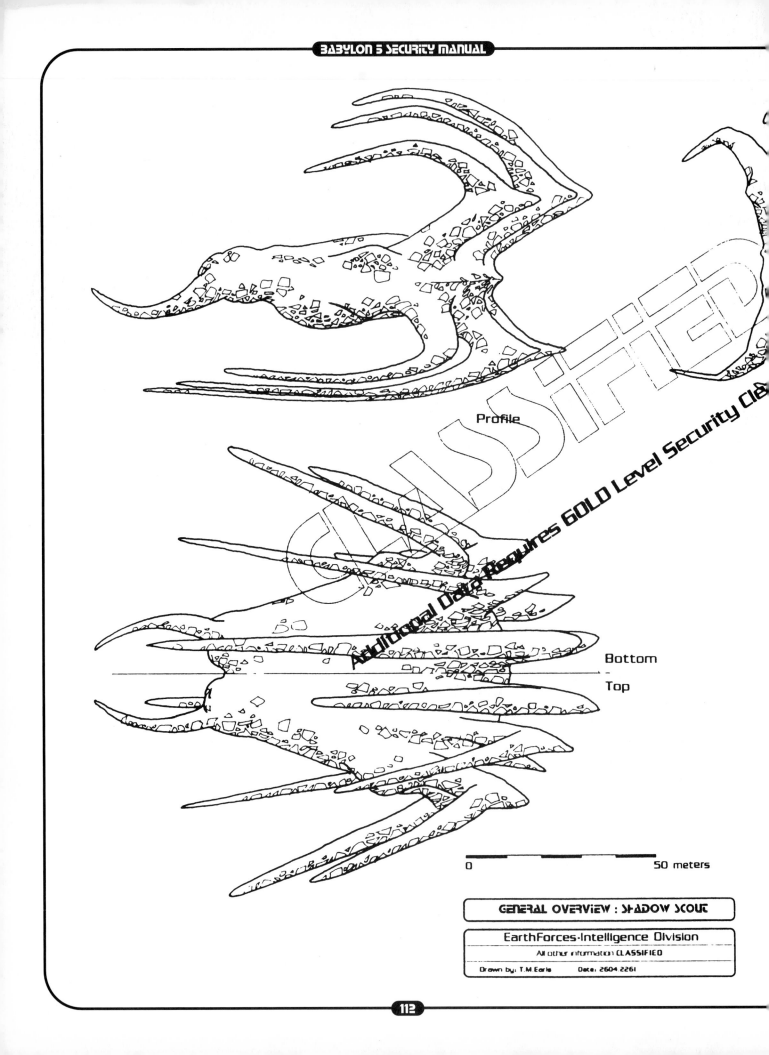

Profile

CLASSIFIED

Additional Data Requires GOLD Level Security Clea...

Bottom

Top

0   50 meters

GENERAL OVERVIEW : SHADOW SCOUT
EarthForces·Intelligence Division
All other information CLASSIFIED
Drawn by: T.M.Earle   Date: 2604 2261

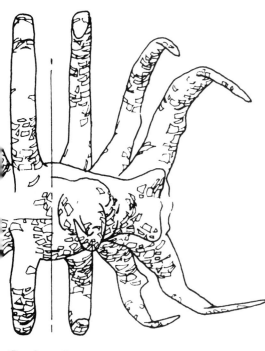

Back   Front

Shadow ships in action

Minbari-Shadow conflict

*Shadow ship
excavated from Mars*

*Shadow ships
destroying Narn base*

*Icarus expedition rover,
which rediscovered the
Shadows after their
1,000-year sleep*

*Icarus on
Za'ha'dum*

unit 7

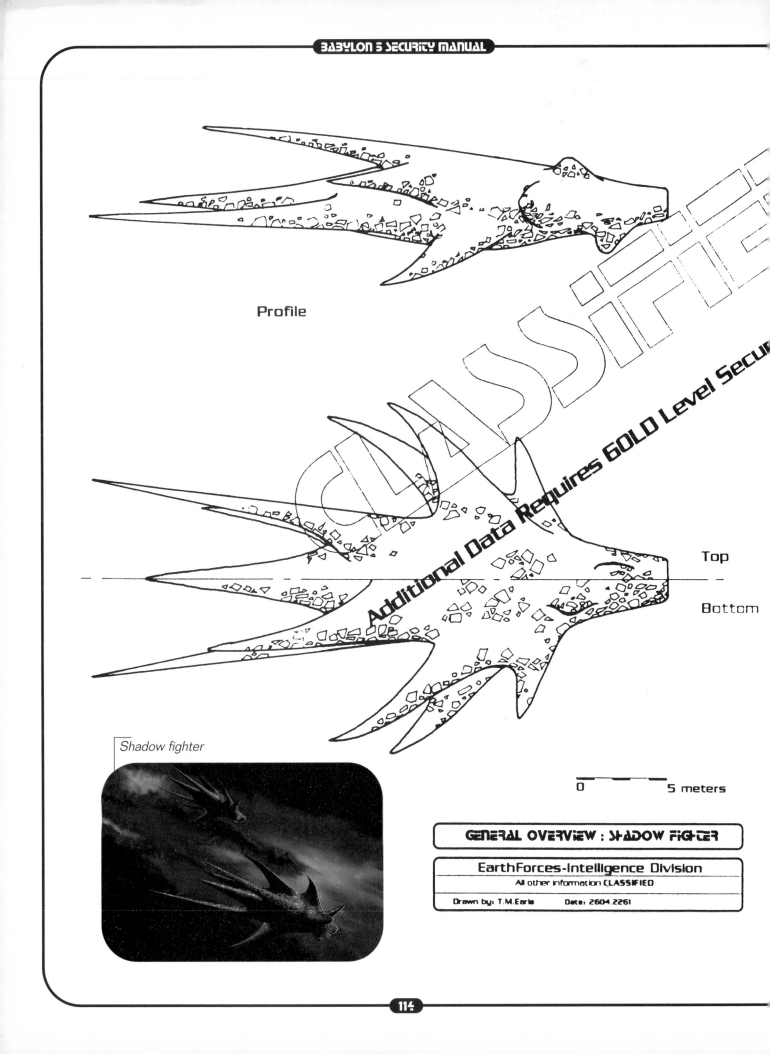

Profile

CLASSIFIED

Additional Data Requires GOLD Level Secu...

Top

Bottom

Shadow fighter

0 ————— 5 meters

GENERAL OVERVIEW : SHADOW FIGHTER

EarthForces-Intelligence Division
All other information CLASSIFIED

Drawn by: T.M.Earle   Date: 2604.2261

Front | Back

arance

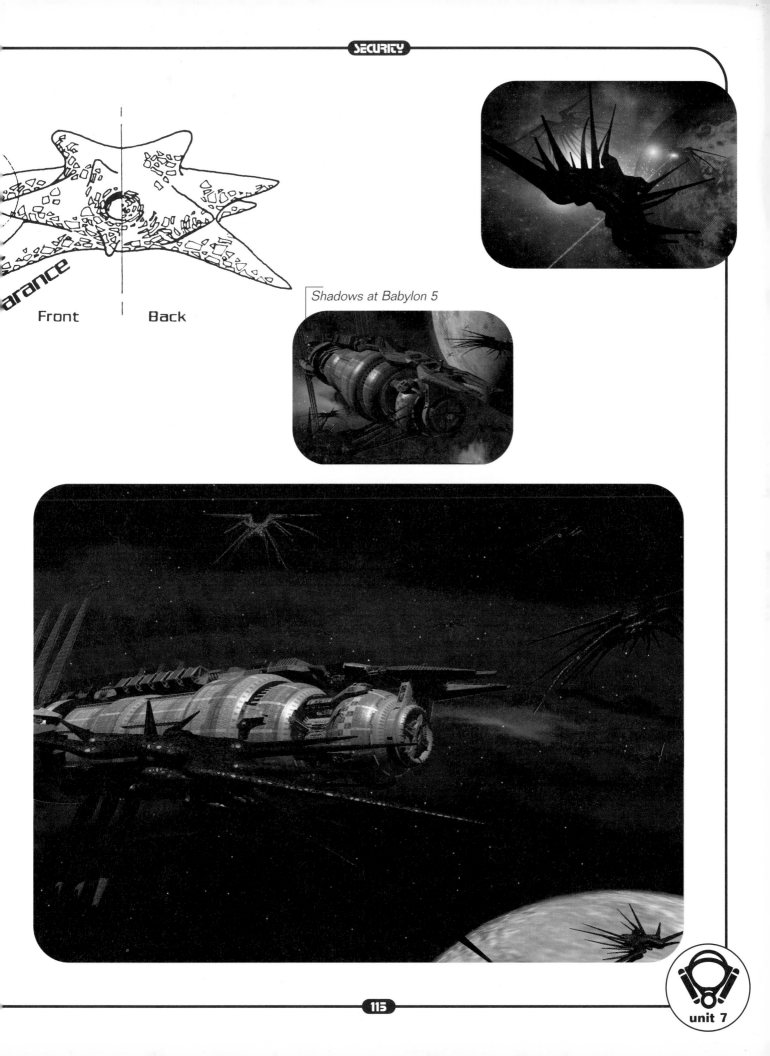

Shadows at Babylon 5

unit 7

7.10 GENERAL

Alien Science Probe

This was a "berserker" probe that appeared off-station a year or so back. It was sent out to find other intelligent species that may prove to be a threat and destroy them. The probe's origins remain unknown.

Alien science probe at B5

Draal and the >>CLASSIFIED<<

The Great Machine is an advanced alien technology that is at the heart of Epsilon 3 and is controlled by a custodian.

A creature called Varn controlled the >>CLASSIFIED<< in a symbiotic relationship until he had to be replaced by Draal, a Minbari. The symbiotic nature of the >>CLASSIFIED<< allows Draal to see all that is said and all that happens, past, present, or future. He can touch the edge of the universe with his thoughts.

Various alien races, including the EA, tried to claim the >>CLASSIFIED<< but Draal warned them that the place belonged to no one and that anyone attempting to land would be destroyed by a powerful defense grid.

There are a number of creatures on the planet, including Zathras and his eleven brothers. Draal is allied with Babylon 5. The >>CLASSIFIED<< alliance remains unknown.

The White Star Fleet

The White Star vessels are an amalgam of Minbari and Vorlon technology, using a revolutionary ship design.

　　　The original *White Star* was given to Captain Sheridan in 2260 at the start of the growing battle against the Shadows, and a fleet was later built by the Minbari for use by the Rangers in the Shadow War.

　　　They are staffed by members of the Minbari religious caste and have artificial gravity and onboard jumpgate technology.

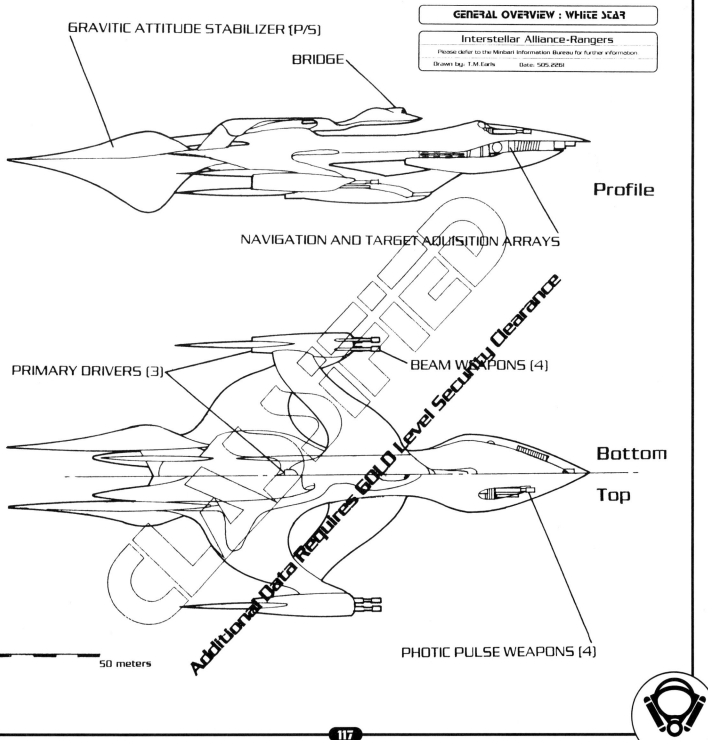

GRAVITIC ATTITUDE STABILIZER (P/S)

BRIDGE

GENERAL OVERVIEW : WHITE STAR
Interstellar Alliance-Rangers
Please defer to the Minbari Information Bureau for further information
Drawn by: T.M.Earls　　　Date: 505.2261

Profile

NAVIGATION AND TARGET AQUISITION ARRAYS

PRIMARY DRIVERS (3)

BEAM WEAPONS (4)

Bottom

Top

0 　　　　　 50 meters

PHOTIC PULSE WEAPONS (4)

Additional Data Requires GOLD Level Security Clearance

unit 7

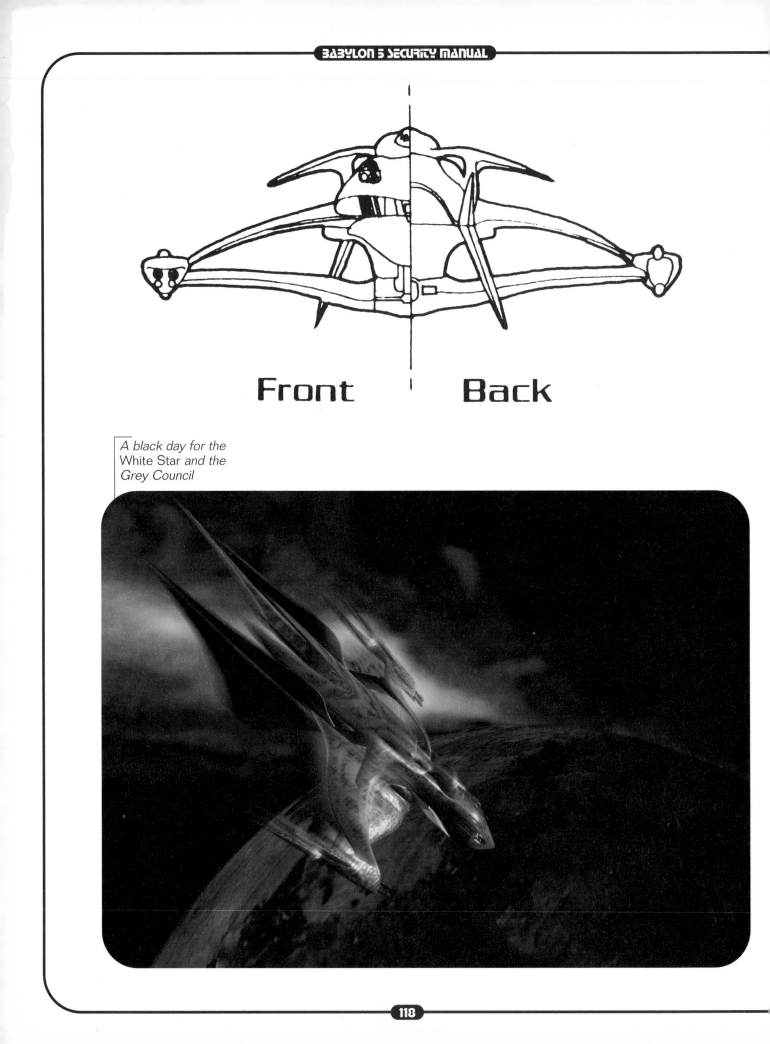

Front   Back

A black day for the White Star *and the* Grey Council

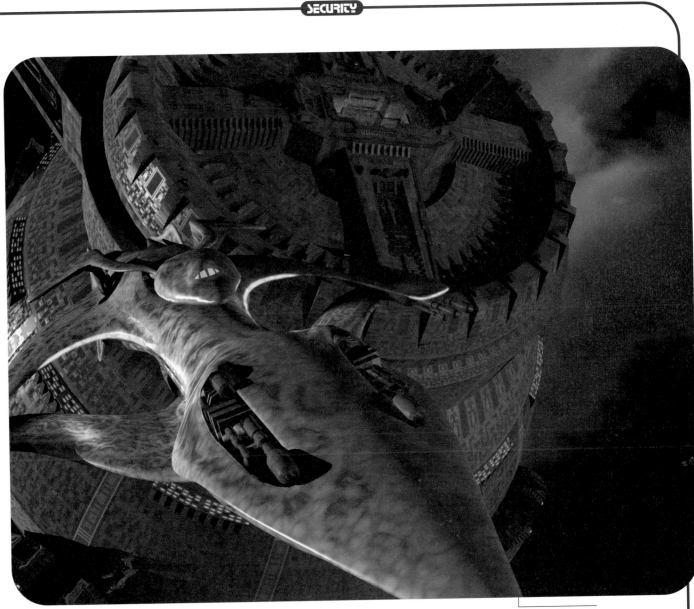

White Star *at Babylon 5*

White Star *at Z'ha'dum*

White Star *on patrol*

unit 7

Babylon 5 is unique in terms of Security, as it has drawn the attention of virtually all known covert operations. Due to its strategic value and high public profile, Babylon 5 makes an ideal target.

This unit will deal with the agencies with which you will be expected to be familiar. Some are dubious, some are classed as terrorist organizations, and others are covert operations set up by the station.

SECTION ONE
8.1 PSI CORPS

All races apart from the Narn have telepaths. The Narn telepaths were wiped out by the Shadows in their first war.

Telepathy has been described as "being in a hotel room where you can just hear the people next door." For telepaths it is always there, even if they try shutting it out, so there are certain rules governing the use of their abilities.

They do not eavesdrop unless invited to. Casual thoughts are easy to block but strong emotions are not. The stronger the telepath is, the easier it is to "listen to the voices" but the harder it is to block them out. The closer you are to a telepath, the easier it is for the telepath to read your thoughts.

A telepathic "attack" consists of pushing mental "buttons" to stimulate someone's memory. Attacks last a second or two and can be quickly shrugged off. However, there are other forms of attack that can stimulate pain centers in the brain.

Information in any person's mind is subjective; it is easier for a telepath to get straightforward information through visual and auditory impulses not overtly open to coloring by subjective aspects.

If a person is unbalanced when scanned, the telepath will be uncomfortable and will see colors, hallucinations, and delusions. Only well-trained telepaths can cope with unbalanced personalities.

Forced telepathic scans can be painful to someone sensitive to psionics. Scans also can be used for good purposes, for instance, to adjust or repair painful or damaged memories.

Sleepers

"My mother was a telepath. Psi Corps used to come around and force her to take the drugs. It messed her up. It messed us all up. My brother went to war and got himself killed, and I never spoke to my father for twenty years. My mother took her own life, and I blame those jackbooted born-with-a-silver-spoon Psi Corps sons of . . . No. I take it back. They never had mothers. Not one of them. They came out of test tubes. Dirty test tubes, crawling with the kind of viruses that make Ebola look like your best damn friend, and they killed my mama! Anyway, I don't want to talk about it. I've got work to do, so move it along there!"

—Susan Ivanova,
Station Second in Command

Only one in a thousand Humans has telepathic abilities, so telepaths are a minority. Full-blown telepaths were discovered 125 years ago (between 2100 and 2110). There were attempts to legislate around this, but they failed.

The foundations for Psi Corps were laid in 2125 by EA president Robinson after his life was saved by a telepath. In 2150 the government agencies that regulated and oversaw telepaths were combined to form Psi Corps—a clearinghouse for locating and licensing telepaths for commercial and military purposes. Psi Corps was officially created as it is today in 2161, when the Greek letter psi (Ψ) was adopted.

The Corps is mother, the Corps is father

Genetic tests were brought in to check for genes present or other recessive abilities. A law was passed that mandated that all telepaths had to contact the Corps, resulting in the vast majority of Psi Corps members being inducted at an early age.

There are various restrictions in place determining the use of telepathy. There should be no unauthorized scans, and the permission of the person (written, dictated, or given by the next of kin) should be obtained. There are few exceptions.

Telepaths are not allowed to "dip," or go into memory zones that are not relevant to the allowed scan. They are also banned from gambling.

Psi Corps itself is forbidden from taking a political stance or endorsing candidates.

Telepaths are forbidden to emphasize intense sensations such as love or pain to coerce cooperation.

All Psi Corps members wear the symbol when among nontelepaths, having been inducted from an early age, when they are assigned a senior trainer in the first year at the academy and taught that "the Corps is mother, the Corps is father."

If a telepath refuses to join the Corps, he or she is forced to take drugs to suppress his or her abilities. These regular injections are called sleepers.

There is a Corps-sponsored "work program" so that the Corps knows what telepaths are doing in society. They serve the business community, the military, and some government agencies. Telepaths can never leave the Corps.

In criminal cases, Psis are not allowed to scan defendants before or during a trial to determine guilt or innocence, as this violates the due process of the law. A Psi may scan the victim of an attack to reveal details, but this information must be backed up by physical evidence; otherwise it is inadmissible in court. Telepaths who operate for the courts are referred to in Psi communities as teeps.

Telepaths have different ratings; the higher the number, the more skilled the telepath and the more abilities the telepath has at his or her disposal. P5s need a little help with scanning (e.g., they need to be near the target).

unit 8

Psi Corps Ratings

The ratings are based on test results and examinations of a person's skills over time in which a person is given training and is constantly interviewed.

Psi ratings vary only slightly; for instance, a P5 can be made into a P6. However, there are more lower ratings, and the higher Ps are very rare. The general rating ranges from one to twelve.

P1   Minimal—do not officially belong, as the skills are of no real value. They are tracked and logged for genetic purposes.

P2   Not much better. They are also tracked and logged.

P3   The Corps considers these persons worth detailed surveillance.

P4   Have to become members of the Corps. They can then be trained to be P5s.

P5   Commercial telepaths. They can detect deception and other surface thoughts. The trick is to bring the thoughts out. They can scan fairly accurately without physical contact. If a person is somehow shielded or a P5 has a court order to perform a deeper scan, they require physical contact to "ground" them. Deeper probing is possible but difficult. Business transactions are the most common use for P5s, as they lack the power or training to determine if memory is altered. Training to the level of P5 is tough. Most of those who train burn out, and some become brain-dead.

P6–9 Military and government telepaths. Used for intelligence.

P10   The upper level of Psi Corps training. They can observe the mental actions of other telepaths and block some scans. They can cut through some blocks and perform long-range scans, and many have some fringe skills. P10s can scan you easily from across the room. A handful of P10s can perform telekinesis, but they are rare and the ability is unstable.

P11   Administration.

P12   Psi Cops. They can communicate with "normals" via telepathy. P12s can scan P5 levels, although two may be required. P12 is the upper limit, and anything above it is a rarity.

Rogue Telepaths

There have been many cases of rogue telepaths coming through Babylon 5 and being chased by Psi Corps on the way.

Some leave Earth due to the regulations governing their use and control (see "Sleepers"). Others tell of atrocities conducted by Psi Corps. These stories include examples of a "forced breeding program" used to supposedly produce telepaths higher than P12.

Jason Ironheart was a P10 instructor. He was experimented on to increase his Psi powers. Genetic and biochemical modifications eventually turned him into a different life-form. He induced telekinesis in his former lover/student Talia Winters.

Ironheart "becoming"

Matthew Stoner was a free trader who traveled across the galaxy. He was an ex-member of Psi Corps who resigned after losing his powers during an experiment. However, his powers were altered, turning him into an empath able to dominate the will of those around him. He was assigned to Talia Winters in the first year at the Psi Corps Academy, and they were married for a short time when they were deemed genetically compatible. When he left the Corps, his marriage was annulled.

Talia Winters herself was subject to covert Psi Corps operations. She was programmed with another personality that would be triggered by a telepathic code. Her job was to spy on the command staff and report back to Earth.

Traitor unmasked: Talia Winters proved to be part of a covert Psi Corps operation

Telepaths were used by the Vorlons to some degree, with resident telepath Lyta Alexander being altered by them in many ways. Telepaths were instrumental in the war against the Shadows. Led by Lyta Alexander, onetime commercial telepath and aide to Vorlon ambassador Kosh, telepaths from all races were instrumental in driving back the Shadow forces in the last months of the war.

Lyta also helped control the actions of Shadow-altered telepaths during the battle to liberate Mars. Many of these telepaths are still in stasis in Babylon 5's medlab.

Refined Telepathic Headgear

The Refined Telepathic Headgear was designed to amplify weak telepathic signals. Originally intended to enhance the abilities of the lower-rated Psi Corps members, the RTH has found considerable use in the commercial marketplace.

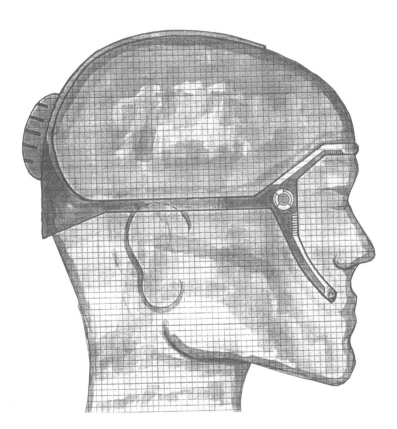

unit 8

*The Psi Corps
headquarters on Earth*

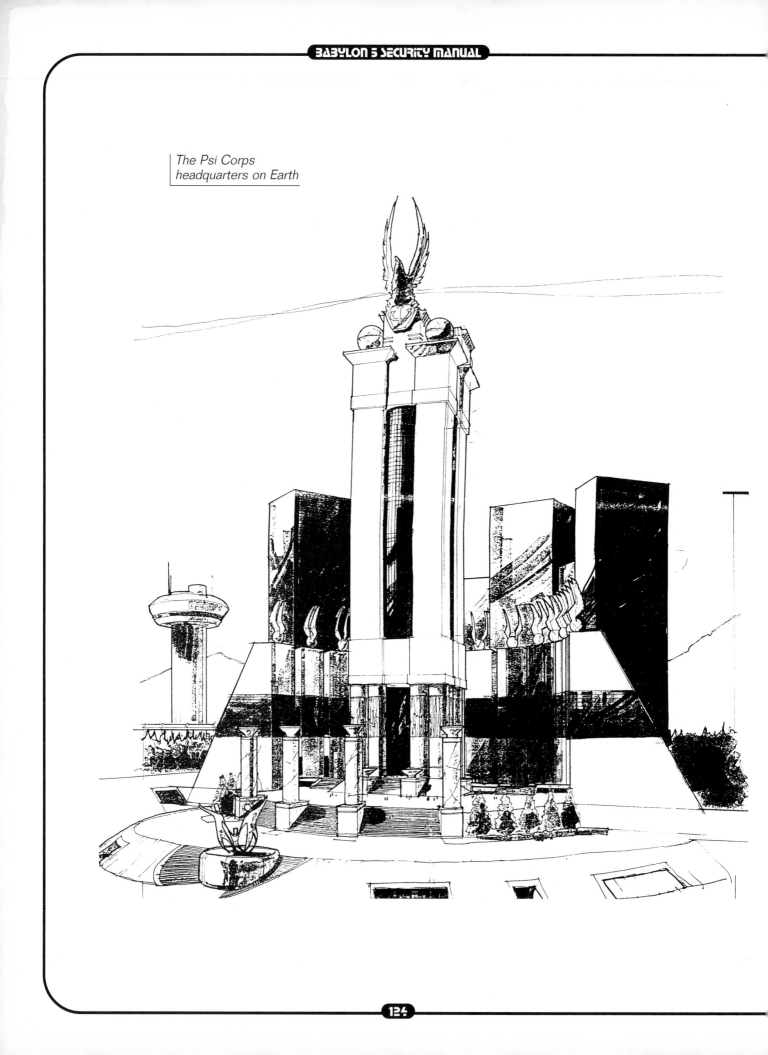

Psi Cops

These are Psionic police and were set up to "watch the watcher." They are telepaths with the highest Psi level, P12, and they monitor and control telepaths.

They are authorized to carry firearms and are allowed more latitude. They wear black uniforms.

Bester

You will, no doubt, at some point in your duties come across the Psi Cop Mr. Bester on one of his infrequent visits to the station.

Do not trust him. He must be watched at all times. If you are in Customs when he comes through, he is to be escorted straight to the brig.

Mr. Alfred Bester

"Be seeing you."

Bester confronted by Sheridan and by Minbari telepaths

unit 8

Underground Railroad

The Underground Railroad is an organization that helps telepaths fleeing the Psi Corps reach the outer colonies. Dr. Franklin is still an organizer and a contact for the rogues entering Babylon 5.

Many other physicians were involved, and Psi Corps traced the railroad to the station. When Bester came onboard to investigate the railroad, his plan was foiled by Talia Winters and her increased psychic abilities.

After that time she was found to be suffering from a deep-personality implant, another kind of "sleeper." Since Talia's mind death her original personality has been reinstated, and she now works for Psi Corps. (Allegedly—there have been rumors that she is dead.) Because of this we must now assume that the Psi Corps knows about the railroad and all who have been involved in it.

Underground Railroad

"Some of the things Psi Corps did I didn't agree with. They were torturing other telepaths. It was thanks to the Babylon 5 Underground Railroad links that I was able to leave it all behind and start a new life. When the call went out for telepaths in the battle against the Shadows, I was only too grateful to help."
—Lee Thacker, Ex–Psi Corps

8.2 BLACK OMEGA SQUADRON

B lack Omega is an EA interceptor squadron consisting of modified Starfuries equipped with stealth capabilities. Black Omega is one of EA's best kept secrets.

It is an infiltration unit involved with black projects and covert missions. The squad is made up mainly of telepaths.

Black Omega
Squadron

unit 8

SECTION TWO— BLACK OPERATIONS

The Rangers

See under "Conspiracy of Light," below.

The Homeguard

The Homeguard is a pro-Earth group that opposes all relations with aliens. There have been various attacks on aliens on the station from the Homeguard, including branding, killing, and kidnapping.

Anyone found to be a member of the Homeguard is to be reported and deported.

Knights One & Two

The Knights were members of a radical Earth group that tried to prove collusion between Earth and Minbar in the war. They came aboard B5 to try to discover what had happened to Commander Sinclair during the Battle of the Line.

Knight Two entered his mind via Cybernet and was brain-damaged when Sinclair broke free and smashed the equipment. Radical groups like this will see Babylon 5 as a target.

Nightwatch

Nightwatch was set up on the direct orders of President Clark and the Ministry of Peace.

Contrary to its "propaganda," Nightwatch acted against the law, but with the blessing of Earth. On Babylon 5 they were involved in an assassination attempt on the Minbari ambassador, Delenn.

After the declaration of martial law, Nightwatch tried to take control of Security so that it could arrest the command staff. This was thwarted, and Nightwatch was banned from the station. All Nightwatch members were sent back to Earth. Nightwatch comes under the Ministry of Peace Intelligence Committee, which reports directly to the president. See Section Three for organization, extracts from the Nightwatch Act, and the Nightwatch Declaration.

Senate Committee on Nightwatch Under President Clark

"Nightwatch's task is the defense of Earth as a whole from external and internal dangers arising from attempts at espionage and sabotage and from the actions of persons and organizations, whether directed from within or from without the planet, that may be judged subversive to the administration."
—Paul Simpson, Committee Member

"Yeah, man, we gotta kick out the subversives."
—Adam Allan, Security Officer

"Nightwatch IS the damn subversives. It's just they don't know it."
—Captain John Sheridan, CO, Babylon 5

Nightwatch is probably an operation formed from ideas hatched by Bureau 13 (see below). (For further information on Nightwatch, see pages 133–136.)

Pierce Macabee,
Nightwatch coordinator,
now banned from
the station

Bureau 13

Bureau 13 was an extremely dangerous covert and rogue element in EA government and was linked with President Clark. Its control was believed to be in the San Diego wastelands, and it was known to have easy access to com systems and Babylon 5 computers.

Bureau 13 was responsible for the death of Taro Isogi, stirring up Homeguard activities, the assassination attempt on the president (with the cooperation of Vice President Clark), and the Jason Ironheart incident.

The assassination of the president was kept secret back home on Earth and was one of the reasons offered for banning travel to and from Babylon 5. The former chief, Garibaldi, found out about the plot to kill the president but was shot by his senior Security officer, Jack. Jack was later sent home on a presidential order.

Bureau 13 was the Earth front for the Shadows, who have systematically changed the political situation on Earth with President Clark backing them all the way. It was their idea to reconstitute the Senate and set up the Committee on Anti-Earth Activities.

Minbari

Most Minbari "black operations" will originate from the warrior caste, not the religious one. However, the religious caste was involved with Babylon 5 in the Conspiracy of Light (see below). A member of the Minbari warrior caste was responsible for the

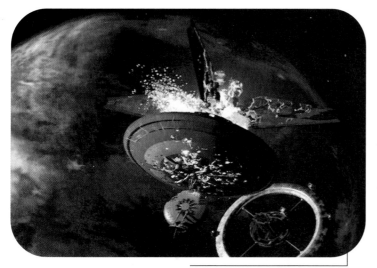

EarthForce 1 *destroyed*

The Able Horn Incident

Able Horn was a Free Mars terrorist and a friend of Amanda Carter. He was responsible for seventy-five terrorist atrocities, including the destruction of Richie Station. He was previously sentenced to one year in the Phobos Maximum Security Outpost in 2252 for the theft of fifty million credits from the Mars Conglomerate, before being transferred to Lunis Planum Prison Base. He escaped on April 15, 2253, and was thought to have been killed over Phobos during the rebellion on Mars in late 2258. His body was in fact rescued and taken in by Bureau 13 and run through Project Lazarus. He was given a mechanical hand capable of massive electrical discharge, with which he killed Taro Isogi. He was able to download things he had seen into the communications system. Talia Winters was able to awaken enough of his original personality to get him to give up his mission and finally provoke Security into killing him. His computer access code was Alpha-6-6-Zeta-3 EF Intelligence File I/6538.

unit 8

assassination attempt on the Vorlon ambassador Kosh when he first came aboard Babylon 5. This was part of the plot to have Commander Sinclair tried for the murder.

A plot involving the religious caste came to light when Captain Sheridan was attacked by a Minbari and set up for murder. This was in retaliation for his appointment on the station after he destroyed their flagship in the Earth-Minbari War.

Finally, a rogue Minbari ship, the *Trigati*, refused to surrender in the Earth-Minbari War and later tried to use Babylon 5 as the staging area for another war before its captain committed suicide in a holding cell.

Luckily, these actions were not "authorized" by the ruling body of the Minbari at the time, the Grey Council, and as such can be seen in isolation rather than as part of Minbari policy. However, future attacks involving the warrior caste cannot be overlooked, especially with Delenn and the station being directly involved in the breakup of the original Grey Council.

Centauri and Narn Operations

Once more, there are no official operations directed against Babylon 5 from these races.

However, the station has been drawn into their conflicts, with both sides funding and arming Raiders and the Centauri gunrunning through local space.

After Captain Sheridan gave sanctuary to a damaged Narn war cruiser, there was an attempt on his life by an unknown Centauri. The Centauri were also supportive of the Shadow attacks.

The Narn Escape Route

One of the more unusual "black operations" onboard Babylon 5 involved Vir Cotto, the Centauri aide.

He did not agree with Centauri policy on Narn, and so he set up his own escape route, helping to get refugees from their homeworld by altering records to say they were dead.

Once this was discovered by command personnel, he was helped by some of the command staff. With the war over, this can safely be revealed; although some Centauri are not pleased, his position in the new order protects him from criticism.

*Destructi
Centauri*

Mollari at the invasion of the Narn homeworld

Destruction of a
Centauri cruiser

A Narn ship destroys
a Centauri ship

Narn versus Centauri,
securecam image

unit 8

The Conspiracy of Light

The Conspiracy of Light is a group consisting of the Rangers, the Babylon 5 command staff, Delenn, G'Kar, and the War Council. Basically, it is the forces of good operating against the Shadows and, of course, lately the Vorlons. It has bases on many worlds, such as the Rangers' training base on Zaymo 3.

The Rangers are field operatives, reporting information back from all corners of the known universe. The Rangers are also trained in fighting techniques and piloted the White Star Fleet in the Shadow War.

The station operates as a base for the Forces of Light where information is gathered and assessed and action is taken. Until now, all information gathered was on the Shadows (the great force of darkness in the universe).

With the war over, the role of the Rangers and Babylon 5 is being reassessed. Mankind is now entering its third age, in which it has been given the task of caring for and guiding the younger races, and this may be a role for the Conspiracy of Light; however, there may still be Shadow agents around to be watched.

The Centauri Ministry of Intelligence has been operating on the station. The Ministry could well be behind a new initiative against Babylon 5.

In 2260, as you know, a presidential mandate was passed preventing any Earth ship from traveling to or from Babylon 5. Any ship violating this order can be seized, and the passengers and crew will be subject to arrest. This was an attempt to isolate Babylon 5 as part of an offensive against us. Phase one was a propaganda war with ISN at the forefront. Phase two was thwarted by us when there was an attempt to frame Babylon 5 forces in Sector 49, site of an EarthForce squadron at the local jumpgate base. This is the last stopover point for ships from Earth before they reach the station. The local Starfury squadron had been ordered to stop and challenge any ships there. The Black Omega Squadron (answerable only to President Clark) was ordered to hide on a transport ship and attack the local Starfuries when challenged. After the patrol was destroyed, evidence was to be left suggesting that Babylon 5 forces had destroyed it. Luckily, this information was passed to us, and a squadron was dispatched to protect the jumpgate.

Rangers

The Rangers have a specific blue gem set in metal that is their means of identification (download this from the computer). They must be given full access at all times.

"I felt it was my duty to become a Ranger. I went through all the tough training, but it was worth it. I was under the command of Marcus in the battle at Coriana 6, and I feel proud to be a Ranger!"
—Brian Cooney, Ranger

Lyta bleeding from the eye during an incursion into Shadow space

Kosh, Sheridan, and Delenn consult on the status of Shadow activity

SECTION THREE—NIGHTWATCH ORGANIZATION

The Nightwatch Act & Declaration

The Nightwatch Intelligence Committee reported directly to President Clark and was the main instrument for advising on intelligence gathering and assessing the results (and dangers thereof) from the Nightwatch via the Ministry of Peace.

The committee set the intelligence requirements and produced assessments on a range of situations and issues. The members of the committee were unknown, but it is believed that it consisted of representatives from Bureau 13, the Ministry of Peace, and Psi Corps.

It met weekly in EarthDome with attendance by the president at a separate briefing. The committee was supported by permanent assessment staff, a secretariat, and a number of specialist interdepartmental subcommittees.

The committee's principal collection agencies passing on information included Nightwatch members, a Shadow secretary, a San Diego listening post, and outer world stations. High priority was given to any anti-Earth actions or those that threatened allies.

The president was responsible for intelligence and security matters overall and was supported in that capacity by the secretary to EarthDome. He was advised on appropriate policy changes by the committee. The committee also was responsible for coordinating interdepartmental plans for intelligence activity and countering any threats where appropriate.

President Clark, address to the Senate, 2260: "This planet is well served by the Ministry of Peace and, indeed, Nightwatch. I was pleased to hear recently that progress has been made on remedying the deficiencies in our interplanetary policy, and I agree with the committee that there is a need for continued vigilance to ensure that intelligence is disseminated in a timely and accurate manner. It is a valuable task that the committee fulfills, and I express my gratitude to them and their colleagues."

unit 8

Section 3 of the Official Nightwatch Act 2060
WRONG COMMUNICATION, etc., of information

1   If any person having in his possession or control any secret official code word, password, sketch, plan, model, article, note, document, or information that relates to or is used in a prohibited place or anything in such a place, or that has been made or obtained in contravention to the best interests of Earth, or that has been entrusted in confidence to him by any person holding office under EarthForce or that he has obtained or that he has had access to owing to his position as a person who holds or has held office under EarthForce, or as a person who holds or has held a contract made on behalf of EarthForce, or as a person who is or has been employed under a person who holds or has held such an office or contract, or is of Earth origin,

(a)   communicates the code word, password, sketch, plan, model, article, note, document, or information to any person, other than a person to whom he is authorized to communicate it, or a person to whom it is in the interest of the president as his duty to communicate it, or;

(b)   uses the information in his possession for the benefit of any alien government or in any other manner prejudicial to the safety or interest of the president;

(c) retains his sketch, plan, model, article, note, or document in his possession or control when he has no right to retain it or when it is contrary to his duty to retain it or fails to comply with all directions issued by lawful authority with regard to the return or disposal thereof, or;

(d) fails to take reasonable care of, or so conducts himself as to endanger the safety of, the sketch, plan, model, article, note, document, secret official code or password or information: then that person shall be guilty of a misdemeanor.

1(A) If any person having in his possession or control any sketch, plan, model, article, note, document, or information that relates to munitions of war communicates it directly or indirectly to any alien power, or in any other manner prejudicial to the safety or interest of Earth, that person shall be guilty of a misdemeanor.

1(B) If any person receives any secret official code word, password, sketch, plan, model, article, note, document, or information, knowing, or having reasonable ground to believe, at the time when he receives it, that the code word, password, sketch, plan, model, article, note, document, or information is communicated to him in contravention of this Act, he shall be guilty of a misdemeanor, unless he proves that the communication to him of the code word, password, sketch, plan, model, article, note, document, or information was contrary to his desire.

1(C) If any person passes comment on policy relating to Earth that is contrary to Earth interests, be this in the form of spoken word, posters, or subversive alien material, that person shall be guilty of a misdemeanor.

unit 8

Nightwatch Declaration

The following legal document had to be signed by all Nightwatch personnel.

Form EAN.05
NIGHTWATCH ACT

Declaration: To be signed by members of Nightwatch on appointment and, where desirable, by noncivilian servants on first being given access to Earth technology and culture.

My attention has been drawn to the provisions of the Nightwatch Act and all relevant anti-Earth activity acts set out on the back of this document, and I am fully aware of the serious consequences that may follow any breach of those provisions.

I understand that the sections of the Act set out on the back of this document cover material published in a speech, lecture, or radio or televisual communication of any form, or in the press, or in book form, link, or computer form. I am aware that I should not divulge any information gained by me as a result of my appointment to any unauthorized person, either orally or in writing, without the previous official sanction in writing from the Ministry of Peace, to which written application should be made and two copies of the proposed publication be forwarded.

I understand also that I am liable to be prosecuted if I publish without official sanction any information that I acquire in the course of my tenure in an official appointment (unless it has already been officially made public) or retain without official sanction any sketch, plan, model, article, note, poster, or official documents that are no longer needed for my official duties, and that these provisions apply not only during the period of my appointment but also after my appointment has ceased. I also understand that I must surrender any documents, etc., referred to in Section 3(1) of the Act if I am transferred from one post to another, save such as have been issued to me for my personal retention.

Signed:

Nightwatch Officer

With the ending of the Shadow War and the liberation of Earth, things on Babylon 5 are getting back to as near "normal" as possible.

Security has a huge part to play in the future, and we should be on our guard against the usual crimes, such as smuggling, theft, murder, etc., and the continuation of "black operations."

It is these acts that will pose the biggest threat to peace on and off the station. Babylon 5 has a higher profile now than it has ever had before and, as such, is bound to be the focus of further "attacks" from these organizations.

Security will need to be tight for occasions similar to the captain's wedding and for the various alien negotiations resulting from recent events—most notably the formation of the Alliance.

There are bound to be "attacks" of one form or another over the coming year, and any suspicious activity must be reported immediately.

Even though Earth may have been liberated, threats may come directly in the form of EarthForce military action or through covert means (provoking alien governments through organizations such as the Homeguard, planting bombs, recording further anti–Babylon 5 propaganda, or sending telepaths to undermine the day-to-day running of the station).

The possibility of new hostilities between the Centauri and the Narn remains a constant that we cannot afford to ignore.

Finally, the Shadows seem to have had allies (a group of them were seen leaving Z'ha'dum before it exploded). Retaliation for our victory in the war is a distinct possibility.

Endgame?

"Hold on to your hats. It ain't over till the fat lady sings."—MG

UNIT 9: CONCLUSION

Babylon Public Safety Communications Officers' Officially Recommended Codes

Standard Codes

4-1 Cannot understand your message

4-2 Your signal is good

4-3 Stop transmitting

4-4 Message received

4-5 Relay information to . . .

4-6 Station is busy

4-7 Out of service

4-8 In service

4-9 Repeat last message

4-10 Negative

4-11 . . . in service

4-12 Stand by

4-13 Report . . . conditions

4-14 Information

4-15 Message delivered

4-16 Reply to message

4-17 En route

4-18 Urgent

4-19 Contact

4-20 Unit location

4-21 Call . . . on BabCom

4-22 Cancel last message

4-23 Arrived at scene

4-24 Assignment completed

4-25 Meet . . .

4-26 Estimated time of arrival is . . .

4-27 Request for information on identicard

4-28 Request credit/identity/room information

4-29 Check computer

4-30 Use caution

4-31 Pick up

4-32 Backup requested

4-33 Emergency situation in . . .

4-34 Correct time

Extended Codes

4-0 Use caution

4-1 Signal weak

4-2 Signal good

4-3 Stop transmitting

4-4   Message received

4-5   Relay information to . . .

4-6   Station is busy

4-7   Out of service

4-8   In service

4-9   Repeat last message

4-10 Fight in progress

4-11 . . . in service

4-12 Stand by

4-13 Report conditions

4-14 Prowler report

4-15 Civil disturbance

4-16 Domestic problem

4-17 Meet complainant

4-18 Urgent

4-19 Go to station

4-20 Advise your location

4-21 Contact . . .

4-22 Disregard

4-23 Arrived at scene

4-24 Assignment complete

4-25 Report to . . .

4-26 Detaining suspect

4-27 Identicard report

4-28 Ambassadorial incident

4-29 Check records for previous records

4-30 Unauthorized use of Gold Channel

4-31 Crime in progress

4-32 Person with weapon

4-33 Emergency—all units stand by

4-34 Riot

4-35 Major crime alert

4-36 Correct time

4-37 War situation alert

4-38 Battle outside station

4-39 Respond with charged PPG

4-40 Do not have weapons ready

4-41 Beginning shift

4-42 End shift

4-43 Information

4-44 Permission to leave

4-45 Dead alien biohazard

4-46 Assist Starfury squad

4-47 Emergency repair crew needed

appendix

4-48 Public access control

4-49 Public access signal out

4-50 Public access incident

4-51 Request command staff presence

4-52 Request medical crew

4-53 Shuttle/transport tube blocked

4-54 Escaped livestock

4-55 Intoxicated pilot in vehicle

4-56 Intoxicated pedestrian

4-57 Gravity problem

4-58 Banned intruder alert

4-59 Escort

4-60 Squad in vicinity

4-61 Personnel in vicinity

4-62 Reply to message

4-63 Prepare to copy

4-64 Local message

4-65 Com message

4-66 Cancel message

4-67 Clear for com message

4-68 Dispatch hard-copy information

4-69 Message received

4-70 Fire alarm

4-71 Advise nature of alarm

4-72 Report progress of alarm

4-73 Smoke report

4-74 Negative

4-75 In contact with . . .

4-76 En route to . . .

4-77 Estimated time of arrival

4-78 Request assistance

4-79 Dead body

4-80 Pursuit in progress

4-81 Toxic gas alert (including oxygen in alien sector)

4-82 Reserve lodgings

4-83 Diplomatic assignment

4-84 Estimated time of arrival

4-85 Arrival delayed

4-86 Operator on duty

4-87 Pick up

4-88 Advise description

4-89 Bomb threat

4-90 Zocalo incident

4-91 Pick up subject

4-92 Illegal substance found

4-93 Battle damage

4-94 Streaker

4-95 Subject in custody

4-96 Detain subject

4-97 Unknown danger

4-98 Prisoner escape

4-99 Wanted or stolen

4-100 Alien interpreter needed

4-105 Deceased person

4-106 Suspicious person

4-107 Check residence

4-108 Customs duty

4-109 Virus alert

4-110 Docking bay duty

4-111 Unauthorized telepath operating

Note here that training is done mainly by Narns. The following schedule is subject to change.

Weeks 1–10

Admin (& general housekeeping—you must know how to do washing & ironing); drill; physical training; weapon training; map reading (star charts & B5 computer maps); Starfuries; first aid & medlab; links; knowing B5 (including recreational areas); B5 history; leadership

Weeks 11–20

Shock stick drill (including riot training); fitness tests (including weightlessness exercise); military aspects of B5; diplomatic relations & etiquette; alien warfare & customs; station & alien law; correct reporting; diplomatic solutions; Customs Area (including Post Office)

Weeks 21–30

The Babylon 5 Treaty; other forces on the station; tactics; use of gas, other weaponry, & recorders; political situations; staff duties; blowouts and evacuations

Weeks 31–34

Weapon training (including field exercises); spacewalking; raiding techniques; one week of tests

Weeks 35–45

Command responsibilities; weapon training; people management; final exercise & pass-out

Weeks 46–47

Counseling; on-the-job experience; specialist training

APPENDIX 2: TRAINING SCHEDULE AND DOCUMENTS

PERSONAL QUALITIES

WEEKS OF TRAINING	Mental Ability	Initiative	Reliability	Physical Ability	Prof. Ability	General Conduct	Unselfishness	L/Ship Potential	Total
1 to 20									
21 to 34									
35 to 47									
TOTALS									

NOTES:

1. Personal qualities are to be graded as follows:
    5 = v good; 4 = good; 3 = average; 2 = below average; 1 = poor.

    However, in areas of doubt the following variations are acceptable:
    5–4.3 = v good; 4.2–3.6 = above average; 3.5–2.6 = average; 2.5–1.8 = below average; 1.8–0 = poor.

2. Each reporting period is to be totaled at the end of the period. On completion of training, final totals are to be calculated.

FINAL ASSESSMENT GRADE

A	B	C	C−	Subject

NOTES:

1. The final assessment grade is produced by totaling the figures.

2. The gradings as related to this overall total are
    A = 270 to 235; B = 234 to 195; C = 194 to 161; C− = 160 to 140.

3. If a C− grade is awarded, the specific subject area must be identified and expanded on in the box below.

TO BE COMPLETED IF A C− GRADE IS AWARDED

SUBJECT	DETAILS

TRAINING RECORD CARD

					JMNW/MNE		TROOP NO/S	

SURNAME & FORENAMES	SERVICE NO	D OF B		REL	B/G	

NEXT OF KIN & ADDRESS

RT		NAMET			
T2					

ENTRY DATE:

FIRST OPT-OUT DATE:

LAST OPT-OUT DATE:

TEL NO

CAREERS OFFICE	B'GROUND	EDUC	STAS	ATT TO AUTH	LEADERSHIP	MOTIV	JOB RCD

OPT OUT: REASONS TO BE GIVEN BY RECRUIT

PHYS	DISCIP	PERS ADMIN	H'SICK	PERS PROBS	UNSUITED	POOR PROSPEC	NO INTEREST	RESTR	OTHER

NOT RECOMMENDED/RECOMMENDED: FOR REENTRY TO: RM/OTHER SERVICES ONLY/ANY SERVICE IN .... MONTHS

appendix

Included for further understanding regarding different situations and the various scales of crime that can happen onboard station. You can access the relevant evidence and complementary case notes on the Security computer.

Accused: Commander Susan Ivanova, Human
Charge: Murder
Victim: J. D. Ortega, suspected Free Mars terrorist
RO: Lois Tilton
Details: Ivanova first brought details of this case to Garibaldi's attention when she reported J. D. Ortega, her former EarthForce flight instructor, missing. She had received a message to meet him, and he did not turn up. When the matter was investigated, the body of Ortega was found in a locker with a message for Ivanova. She became the prime suspect due to the lack of further evidence. Commander Wallace, Lieutenant Miyoshi, and Lieutenant Khatib took control of the investigation after arriving from Earth and placed Ivanova on restricted duties under suspicion of terrorism and conspiracy. Garibaldi found that Ortega had been killed by Yang, an AreTech enforcer. AreTech, a Mars-based mining corporation, had been supplying arms to Raiders. However, before this evidence could come to light, Yang was murdered by Khatib, who in turn was murdered by Wallace in an attempted cover-up. While retrieving evidence left by Ortega in her Starfury, Ivanova was attacked by Miyoshi. Babylon 5 Security officer: the following case notes may be helpful. John Vornholt shot Miyoshi in self-defense, killing her. The evidence found by Ivanova was a data crystal giving details of a new atom, supermorbidium, useful in high-tech weapons systems. After this evidence was passed to Earth and EarthDome investigated charges against AreTech, the case was closed and Ivanova was cleared on all counts.

Accused: Greegil D'Farkin, Narn
Charge: Attempted murder
Victim: Ambassador G'Kar, Captain Sheridan
RO: David Gerrold
Details: Narn Ambassador G'Kar kidnapped Security Chief Garibaldi in an attempt to leave the station quickly. Captain Sheridan set off in pursuit with the accused, but when they caught up with G'Kar's spaceship, it was empty and set for self-destruct. While spacewalking to repair damages, the accused threatened to cut

the survival leads to Captain Sheridan and leave him behind. Luckily, the captain was the only one with the necessary codes to operate the ship. G'Kar and Garibaldi were hiding in the core, where they escaped a cleaning 'bot. The accused had sworn a sacred oath, a Chon-Kar, to kill G'Kar after he refused to mate with a member of his family, thereby forming an alliance between their clans and shifting the Narn balance of power. Greegil was arrested with the use of a Starweb by Officer Gorton upon his return to the station. He was found guilty and sentenced. G'Kar claimed diplomatic immunity on the charge of kidnapping Garibaldi.

Accused: (1) Nelson Drake, Human

(2) Dr. Vance Hendricks, Human

Charge: (1) Murder and smuggling

(2) Accessory to murder and smuggling

Victim: Customs Officer Delgado

RO: Cooper Rowland

Details: Dr. Hendricks and his assistant, Nelson Drake, arrived on Babylon 5 with artifacts from Ikaara 7. A number of "organic" artifacts were smuggled aboard that led to the murder of Officer Delgado. These artifacts were in fact weapons that attached themselves to Drake, genetically changing him. The Drake weapon rampaged through the station, intent on destroying anything that was not pure. Commander Sinclair made the intelligent weapon realize that it had destroyed life on its own planet, at which point it detached itself from Drake. Drake and Hendricks were arrested and brought before the Ombuds.

Accused: Mountpara Rekt, Netzer race

Charge: Theft of ideas

Victim: Nerwar Ltd. (Zyntrakis)

AO: Wendy Ling

Details: The Netzer race has limited telepathic abilities. It is against its laws for ideas of any kind to be stolen and used by others. This law was extended to Babylon 5, which is fast becoming a meeting point for Netzer business negotiations. It has been agreed that the law affects only members of the Netzer race. Philosopher Zyntrakis, working for Nerwar Ltd., was unofficially scanned by Mountpara Rekt. Plans for a space station were duplicated and sold as part of a franchise deal by Rekt. Officer Wendy Ling was present at the time and picked up on the scanning with her telepathic abilities. Mountpara was later charged and denounced back on the Netzer homeworld.

Accused: Orsorb Vinkev, Culesher race
Charge: Carrying weapons banned on the station
AO: Neal Barrett
Details: Orsorb Vinkev was arrested while walking through the Zocalo carrying a number of weapons, both concealed and otherwise. However, the weapons are ceremonial to the Culesher and are hardly ever used due to their great strength. Upon examination, it was found that the weapons were secured on Vinkev's person and could not be removed. Charges were dropped.

Accused: Ambassador Londo Mollari, Centauri
Victim: Icovelli Corporation, owners of Zocalo Bars
Charge: Drunk and disorderly, criminal damage
AO: S. M. Stirling
Details: Officer S. M. Stirling was on patrol in the Zocalo when noise was heard coming from one of the bars. A disheveled Centauri, later identified as Ambassador Londo Mollari, was found lying on the floor singing Centauri opera next to a broken table and chair. Ambassador Mollari was drunk and had been refused further drinks by the management, at which point he had tried to punch one of the barmen but instead fell on the table and chair, breaking them. The following day Ambassador Mollari paid damages in full with compensation for the trouble caused. Charges could not be brought due to diplomatic immunity.

Accused: The Babylon Five, Leets
Victim: Various
Charge: Murder, inciting a riot, use of firearms, dangerous driving, illegal use of weapons and stimulants, mistaken identity, illegal use of sacrificial victim
AO: B Squad
RO: Chris Dunford, Anna Higgins
Details: This is one of the most complicated cases in the history of Babylon 5. The Babylon Five are of the Leet race and as such are not counted by most civilizations as being responsible for their actions. Due to legal difficulties, this case has been going on for three years, and various protest groups have been set up (expect to see the occasional "Free the Babylon Five" T-shirt). One of the Leets was approached by a drug dealer as the Leets were organizing a party to celebrate the Festival of Xotia. They used their own quarters as the venue, and Security received a number of complaints regarding the noise. An officer was sent to investigate. After two hours the officer had not returned. Another two officers were dispatched to investigate and found that the party had spilled onto the rest of the

floor with many Pak'ma'ra in attendance. The original officer had
been sacrificed. The Leets had been awaiting delivery of a sacrificial
creature and mistook the officer for the one ordered. After reporting
in and calling for backup, the two officers were offered drinks by a
passing Narn to calm their nerves. These turned out to be banned
substances and left one of the officers with a mental age of three
and the other unable to use the little finger on his left hand.
Unfortunately, B Squad arrived as the Leet time mechanism struck
fourteen zontons—in Leet legend, at the Festival of Xotia, the evil
Synth will return on the stroke of fourteen. A full-scale battle
ensued until everyone had been arrested. Various banned articles
were retrieved, many were arrested for being "drunk" (or the
species equivalent), and drug dealers using the party were taken
into custody. Two of the Leets escaped on hover boards (also
banned) and were chased through the Zocalo. There they took
shelter in a grocery store before throwing the stock at the arresting
officers. The case continues.

Accused: LoSo Han, Human
Charge: Smuggling
AO: Wendy Ling
Details: LoSo Han was seen exchanging money Down Below with a Drazi.
He returned to his ship and brought back some fingal eggs. He was
arrested on suspicion of smuggling and searched. His ship was
searched, and a number of fingal eggs were found in a hatchway
underneath the floor in one of the ship's corridors. He admitted
smuggling and was fined.

Accused: Malcolm Biggs, Human
Victim: Various aliens
Charge: Homeguard activity
RO: Pen'y Y'Terrier
Details: After a series of attacks on aliens by the Homeguard, it was
revealed that a cell was working from within Babylon 5. Malcolm
Biggs, an ex-lover of Commander Ivanova, revealed his
involvement to her. Commander Sinclair infiltrated the group and
found out that there was a plot to kill the station ambassadors.
Groups on Earth would use this as a signal to kill emissaries there.
The cell was drawn out into the open, arrested, and sent back to
Earth for trial.

Accused: Jinxo, Human
Victim: Aldous Gajic
Charge: Petty theft
AO: Security Chief Garibaldi
RO: Zack Allan
Details: Jinxo was a known petty thief who had been a construction worker on the station. Jinxo was easily led and became involved with the criminal Deuce. Jinxo was caught by the chief stealing from Aldous Gajic. However, due to his simple nature, leniency was suggested at the court. Jinxo believed that if he left the station it would be destroyed, as after he had left previous stations they had been sabotaged. Aldous, the last of a religious order, spoke up for him at his trial, and Ombuds Wellington put him under his supervision. Jinxo led Security to Deuce, and in the ensuing battle Aldous was killed. Jinxo left to take up his quest for the Holy Grail.

Accused: Za'Talef, Pak'ma'ra
Victim: Zolin delegation
Charge: Murder and cannibalism
RO: David Moore
Details: A delegation of five Zolin were onboard the station in negotiations with the Centauri. Za'Talef was seen giving the delegation members a drink before taking them toward his quarters. The Centauri aide Vir Cotto reported the delegation missing after they did not turn up at the negotiations. There was no reply from their quarters. Za'Talef denied knowing or seeing the Zolin and was questioned initially in his quarters, where Officer Moore spotted a Zolin ornament worn around the neck. Za'Talef was arrested but refused to cooperate. After his stomach had been pumped, he admitted to drugging the delegation members before killing and eating them. The remains were later found in the waste disposal system.

Accused: Stuart Sanderson, Human
Victim: Mark Sontar
Charge: Murder
RO: Nigel Parkes
Details: Stuart Sanderson was a petty criminal who had been arrested and charged with theft a number of times. He had no fixed abode and had also been brought up on charges of breach of the peace after arguing with Mark Sontar, a trader from Down Below. There had been many reports of arguments between these two being broken up by Security. It was after one such argument that Mark Sontar was found stabbed four times and dumped by one of the recyclers. Stuart Sanderson was one of those who were routinely questioned.

A few other traders were questioned, and it was found that there had been an argument that morning and that later Sanderson had bought a knife. A search of his quarters produced the weapon, and he was charged.

Accused: Geio Dfkjnon, Clofna
Victim: Dflon Simba
Charge: Petty theft
RO: Terry Skerritt-Morgan
Details: During the Clofna Wrinda, Geio Dfkjnon took a Terioxcvmn from the Wbnod during the Wrim in the Wrinda celebrations. It was used for Slvinging another Clofna but was discovered when Geio was seen putting it on the Wrinda Glovonckle. The item belonged to Dflon Simba, and charges were pressed. (For details on the above ceremonies and Clofna items, look on the computer under the Clofna race.)

Accused: Jane Lowry, Human
Victim: Peter Anderson
Charge: GBH
RO: Gary Ward
Details: Officer Gary Ward was sent out to quarters being shared by Jane Lowry and Peter Anderson after a call from Lowry. She was in an upset state, repeating to herself, "I've killed him, I've killed him." Officer Ward found Mr. Anderson battered and bruised among the wreckage of the quarters. Medlab was called, and Mr. Anderson was treated. Jane Lowry was given a sedative and later admitted battering her partner after finding a Lumati sex toy in his belongings. Security later found that the bag in which it had been found did not belong to Mr. Anderson, and no charges were pressed.

Accused: Bandton Sonack, Human
Victim: Oflav Coobar
Charge: Assault, attempted robbery, resisting arrest
AO: Dave Gorton
Details: Oflav Coobar was walking along Grey 15 when he claimed he was stopped by the accused. He was threatened with a knife, and money was demanded. When Oflav refused, he was punched and kicked to the ground. It was reported within a couple of hours, and a description was passed to all stations. Bandton Sonack was stopped on his way to Down Below, where he attempted to escape custody by pulling a knife. Bandton was identified in a lineup and charged.

Accused: Commander Susan Ivanova, Human
Victim: Various
Charge: Smuggling, buying, cutting, and pushing Red Mountain coffee
Details: Victims would not press charges. Case dismissed.

Accused: Ambassador Londo Mollari, Centauri
Victim: Various
Charge: Drunk and disorderly
Details: Diplomatic immunity. Case dismissed.

Accused: CWO Michael Garibaldi, Human
Victim: Various
Charge: Noise pollution
Details: Offending weapon: Kawasaki motorcycle. Bike impounded.
Fine paid.

Accused: Lennier, Minbari
Victim: Various
Charge: Aiding and abetting
Details: Was guilty of helping to build the Kawasaki bike cited as evidence in
the previous case. Diplomatic immunity. Case dismissed.

Accused: Ambassador G'Kar, Narn
Victim: Ambassador Londo Mollari, Centauri
Charge: Attempted murder
Details: Diplomatic immunity. Case dismissed.

Accused: Ambassador Londo Mollari, Centauri
Victim: Various bar patrons
Charge: Drunk and disorderly
Details: Diplomatic immunity. Case dismissed.

Accused: CMO Stephen Franklin, Human
Victim: Various
Charge: Drug abuse, operating without due care and attention
Details: Franklin's value as surgeon recognized. Released by court under
Rehabilitation Order 9.

Accused: Ambassador Londo Mollari, Centauri
Victim: Adilliyar Nan, Xoatian
Charge: Drunk and disorderly
Details: Diplomatic immunity. Case dismissed.

Accused: Ambassador Londo Mollari, Centauri
Victim: Darren Barnard, bartender, ex–Psi Corps
Charge: Drunk and disorderly, assault with a deadly weapon (accidental)
Details: Darren suffered a fractured skull when struck by a bronze idol of the Centauri god of peace and diplomacy. Ambassador Mollari paid for all medical services when sober, but Darren died during surgery from internal hemorrhaging. The Centauri government cited diplomatic immunity. Case dismissed.

Accused: Captain John Sheridan, Human
Victim: All of sentient life
Charge: Destruction of
Details: Accused by Shadow government via Human representatives. Judicial authority not recognized. Case dismissed.

Accused: Ambassador Londo Mollari, Centauri
Victim: Various
Charge: Drunk and disorderly
Details: Diplomatic immunity. Case dismissed.

Accused: Ambassador Londo Mollari, Centauri
Victim: Various
Charge: Genocide, use of illegal weapons, incitement to war, destruction of property in the value of one planetary economy
Details: Diplomatic immunity. Case dismissed.

appendix

I t is important that you know a bit about the people you work with on a day-to-day basis. Here you will find details about the main crew, ambassadors and their aides, the previous chief of Security, and the Psi Cop Bester.

President John Sheridan

Captain John Sheridan was transferred to Babylon 5 by order of Earth president Santiago. He is now president of the Alliance of Free Worlds.

He was in command of the *Agamemnon* at the time of his assignment to Babylon 5 and was surprised to be transferred due to the hatred the Minbari had of him. He destroyed one of their warships (the *Black Star*) during the Earth-Minbari war, earning him the nickname Starkiller among the Minbari warrior caste. The Grey Council (leaders of the Minbari) protested his appointment, but he was apparently the president's first choice. It did not help that one of his first tasks on Babylon 5 was to guard against a rogue Minbari warship.

Despite worries about the change, Garibaldi and the rest of the staff quickly warmed to him. Ivanova had served under him before, and he quickly promoted her. He is known for his corny jokes and likes making speeches.

His wife Anna was killed out on the Rim in 2257. It was later found that she had been taken over by the Shadows, and they later used this against him. His sister visited him on the station to talk about his wife just after he got the command.

He has a strong sense of right and wrong and will defend his beliefs even if this puts him up against his own superiors or other races. This led him to declare independence from Earth after the controversial policies put forward by Santiago's successor, President Clark.

During the Shadow War, Sheridan enlisted the help of virtually all races and attempted to destroy the Shadows' homeworld, Za'ha'dum. This led to his death and to the discovery of the very first First One, Lorien.

Lorien gave Sheridan life again, and Sheridan came back to the station to organize the final battle. When the Vorlons started attacking, he let out a piece of Kosh, the first Vorlon ambassador, and again died. Lorien brought him back to life a second time.

During the final battle between the allies, the Vorlons, and the Shadows, it was Sheridan who worked it out that the enemies wanted us to choose between the order and the chaos that they stood for. He stood up to them and persuaded them to leave for the Rim. After leading the liberation of Earth, Mars, and the Earth colonies from Clark's rule, Sheridan resigned his commission and was named president of the new Alliance of Free Worlds.

Sheridan has married Ambassador Delenn.

Commander Susan Ivanova

Commander Susan Ivanova comes from the Russian Consortium on Earth and is the station's first officer.

She developed a dislike of Psi Corps after her mother turned out to be a latent telepath and was given drugs to suppress her abilities. Ivanova watched as her mother slowly withdrew from her family and then tragically ended her life. This is one reason for Ivanova's point-blank refusal to be scanned.

She grew away from her father and joined EarthForce. His death raised issues of faith for her. She served with Captain Sheridan before joining the station, and it was Ivanova who met the captain when he was transferred to Babylon 5.

Her dislike of Psi Corps caused her a few problems in the past. She initially hated Talia Winters, the station's commercial telepath, but they grew closer. In her spare time she seems to like reading, drinking coffee, and relaxing in general.

She has worked her way up the ranks on her own merits. A trained and accomplished combat pilot, she has a short temper and a quick wit and is always there with a comment or two.

She was invaluable during the Shadow War, looking after the running of the station when Captain Sheridan did not return from Za'ha'dum. She also managed to find all the remaining First Ones for the final battle and persuade them to join.

After the battle to liberate Earth and Mars, Ivanova left Babylon 5 and was assigned a ship's command.

Security Chief Zack Allan

Surely you must know who I am. If not, come and ask for me in the Security office.

Dr. Stephen Franklin

Dr. Stephen Franklin replaced Babylon 5's first MO, who was recalled to Earth after seeing a Vorlon.

Dr. Franklin is extremely set in his ways. He always puts his work first and for a period of time began relying on stims to be able to continue working, which caused slight friction between himself and Garibaldi.

He was educated at Harvard, gaining good results in alien history, anatomy, and biology, and has a strained relationship with his father, General Richard Franklin.

As you would expect from a doctor, Franklin is extremely ethical and has a high regard for life, be it Human or alien. He even destroyed all his research into the Minbari during the war rather than have it used against them. He has also helped telepaths on the Underground Railroad and regularly does surgery in Down Below.

CWO Michael Garibaldi

Michael Garibaldi is the ex-chief of Security.

He has worked in security off and on for most of his life, although he was fired from previous jobs for unspecified personal problems and sometimes has doubts about his own abilities.

However, he was personally chosen for the job on Babylon 5 by Commander Sinclair. They had met on Mars when Garibaldi was suffering from drinking problems. Garibaldi saved Sinclair's life, and they both encountered a Shadow craft.

It was on Mars that a friend of Garibaldi was killed by a bomb intended for him. This caused Garibaldi to turn to the bottle again after blaming himself. Garibaldi gradually cut off all ties with Mars, even with Lise Hampton, with whom he once had a relationship.

He served as a soldier in the Earth-Minbari War and is a trained pilot and has many other skills. He knows more about life on Babylon 5 than does anyone else. Not much goes on without him knowing about it.

He was injured after finding evidence of an assassination attempt on the Earth president. He has become close to only a few of the residents, notably Ivanova, G'Kar, and Mollari. However, he did have a soft spot for Talia Winters.

He has a great sense of humor and wit and has an interest in motorcycles and cartoons (his second favorite thing in the universe is a Duck Dodgers cartoon!).

He was missing for weeks when the Shadows surrounded the station. On his return, a medic found nothing wrong, but he could not remember anything about the missing time. It was discovered that, during the battle to liberate Earth and Mars, he had been programmed by Psi Cop Bester to betray Sheridan. After making amends and clearing his name, Garibaldi is now the Chief Warrant Officer of the Alliance of Free Worlds.

Ambassador Londo Mollari

Londo Mollari is the assigned ambassador to Babylon 5 for the Centauri Republic after recently becoming its prime minister.

He believes in enjoying himself as much as possible and is frequently seen drinking or gambling. He also enjoys the company of beautiful women.

He yearned for the old days of the republic, when the Centauri dominated large regions of space, and made a deal with the Shadows to reclaim it. This started the war between the Narn and the Centauri.

Obviously, this caused tension on the station between Mollari and others, mainly Ambassador G'Kar of the Narn Regime. The Centauri invaded the Narn homeworld and then pulled out, leaving it virtually barren.

Mollari realized what he did and set about trying to put things to rights. When G'Kar was taken by the Centauri, Mollari managed to set up an elaborate plan to rid Centauri Prime of the Shadows and free G'Kar and his people. When the emperor died, Mollari was left virtually in charge of the Centauri until the Centauri can work out the bloodline and appoint a new emperor.

Mollari's wish is that he will die doing something noble and brave, but it is doubtful that his wife believes he will (he did have three wives but was granted a divorce from two of them by a previous emperor).

Mollari seems to find himself in situations he would rather not be in, usually of his own making. He has admitted to having dreams about the future that have come true.

Ambassador G'Kar

The militaristic Ambassador G'Kar is the Narn Regime's representative on Babylon 5.

After his father was killed by their Centauri master, G'Kar vowed to fight for freedom. He dedicated his life to serving his people ever since, and this has brought him into conflict with others, especially Ambassador Mollari of the Centauri, who once invaded his world.

In his attempts to further his people's cause, he has tried many things, including buying DNA from telepaths and trying to frame others for an attempted Narn assassination of Ambassador Kosh.

Despite his bitterness after the suffering he has seen, he can be a kind person and has helped many, including the planetologist Catherine Sakai.

He is a deeply religious Narn, following the teachings of G'Quan.

appendix

He was a member of the third circle of the Kha'Ri, the Narn ruling body. Over the last few years G'Kar has come to care a lot more for others and has made many sacrifices.

Not the least of these losses was one of his eyes (he now has an artificial one). He lost it when he was caught by the Centauri while searching for Garibaldi and was tortured. He helped Mollari with a plan to rid Centauri Prime of the Shadows and thus free the Narn homeworld.

He was offered a place as "emperor" of Narn but turned it down due to the endless circle of tyranny and counterblame in the Narn-Centauri conflict. He was invaluable during the Shadow War.

Ambassador Delenn

Ambassador Delenn represents the Minbari Federation.

She is a member of the Minbari religious caste and had a position on the Grey Council (the nine leaders of the entire Minbari race). She knew the secret of Kosh's true identity and helped with preparations for the Shadow War.

The Minbari waged their own devastating war against Earth but surrendered on the brink of victory in 2248. Delenn was present when the Minbari examined Jeffrey Sinclair and found that Humans had Minbari souls. Their beliefs prevented them from continuing the war.

Delenn realized that she had a greater part to play in the war against the Shadows and underwent a change to become half-Human and half-Minbari. The idea was to bring Humans and Minbari together, but there were those who believed she had fulfilled an ancient prophecy too early, and she lost her place on the Grey Council.

She later led the allies in the fight against the Shadows and was instrumental in the breaking up of the Grey Council, fulfilling the prophecy of which she had become a part.

She is a kindly figure, always approachable, and is now Captain Sheridan's wife.

Vir Cotto

Vir Cotto is a member of the Centauri and acts as Ambassador Mollari's attaché on Babylon 5. He has recently acquired a high position in the Centauri government.

He sometimes provides amusement for others through his behavior, but he is by no means as stupid as some people, including Mollari, seem to think. He observed what went on between Mollari and Morden and annoyed the latter with his whimsical put-downs. This demonstrated that Vir does not scare easily.

Vir has a strong sense of what is right and acts as a conscience for Mollari. He had no wish to see the republic return to its former glories and was against many aspects of the war effort. He disagrees with many Centauri customs, such as putting power and wealth above love for others.

All his life Vir has been pushed to one side by others, which is how he got to be on Babylon 5. Once Mollari and the station became important to the Centauri, they wanted to replace him but found that he had become an invaluable resource—so much so that when he was to be replaced, Mollari refused to let him go.

He has gained a lot of respect for himself on Babylon 5, among other races, among station personnel, and with the Centauri. He is surely destined for greater things.

Lennier

Lennier is the Minbari aide to Ambassador Delenn.

He did not know how to take her initially due to her position on the Grey Council, but he quickly overcame this. He has tremendous respect for Delenn, and they have become very close. He has stood by her through many difficult situations.

He is a typical member of the religious caste in Minbari society, having been raised in a monastery to become a member of the Third Fane of Chudomo. He has strong beliefs about what is right and wrong and would easily sacrifice himself for others.

He is passionate about history and is more than competent in self-defense. He is always willing to learn about other cultures, sometimes with hilarious results (especially when either Garibaldi or Mollari is involved).

Sheridan finds him invaluable as first officer on the *White Star*.

Psi Cop Bester

Bester embodies the more sinister side of the Psi Corps.

He is a highly trained Psi Cop and will do anything to safeguard telepaths, including killing. It seems that he is always tracking things and people to Babylon 5, usually renegade telepaths.

He is not averse to illegal scans and prefers telepathic communication. With all his experience on Babylon 5, he has slightly warmed to the crew members despite their loathing of him, which they do not try to hide. He is usually forced to cooperate with the crew, which he finds amusing.

One of his loves, another telepath, was sent by the Psi Corps to be used by the Shadows in their vessels. He came to Babylon 5 for help, and we were able to rescue her. However, she has Shadow technology grafted into her and has to be kept in cryogenic suspension until it can be figured out how to remove it.

It is due to this that Bester occasionally helps Babylon 5. However, he is not to be trusted.

appendix

BIBLIOGRAPHY

This book could not have been written without the use of various booklets and information published by HMSO on behalf of HM Government's Security Services.

The Babylon File, Andy Lane, Virgin 1997; *The A-Z of Babylon 5*, David Bassom, Boxtree, 1996; *Cinefantastique; The Making of a Royal Marine Commando,* Nigel Foster, Sidgwick & Jackson, 1987; *Micromachines: Official Secrets*, David Hooper, Secker & Warburg, 1987; *The Politics of the Police,* Robert Reiner, St. Martin's Press, 1985; *The Strong Arm of the Law,* P. A. J. Waddington, Oxford University Press, 1991; various Internet sites, including JMS On-line, the Babylon 5 A-Z, and the Lurker's Guide.

ACKNOWLEDGMENTS

Allan Adams would like to thank Peter Adams, Adrian Rigelsford, Andy Lane, Andrew Pixley, Ryan K. Johnson (for his enthusiasm for B5 [not]), Philip Adams, Carl and Stuart Vandal, Dave Burke, Rob Lowry, Ness Bishop, David Beard, Chris Mayell, Pete Cox, Diane Slater, Taff, Dave Rogers, J. Michael Straczynski, Doug Netter, John Copeland, George Johnsen, Jeffrey Willerth, Craig Ross, Joanne Higgins, John Iacovelli, Mark Walters, Timothy Earls, Alan Kobayashi, Geoff Mark, Tom Helmers.

Roger Clark would like to thank Mum, Dad, Gillian, Glenn Reed, Chris Dunford, Dave Goreon, HMSO, Mick Davies (Cabinet Office), HM Customs & Excise, all at Boxtree, Clive Evans, all involved with Sector 14 & "Fenric," Wendy Ling and all the Southern Shire Unit. Oh, and hello to Julie, Pete, Kevin, Steve, and all at WCR.

Jim Mortimore would like to thank a few people, too. First past the post are Allan Adams and Roger Clark for producing the first Damn Fine draft of this manuscript. Joint first place goes to Trees for *being* Damn Fine. A close second, third, fourth, etc. are Andy and Sue, Phil, Ian and Steve for my new kitchen, Steve and Donna and Darren Paul (and the mysteriously unnamed impending arrival), my family, Finn Clark and all the people who wrote in support of Nakula (MORE LETTERS! I NEED MORE LETTERS!! SEE ETERNITY WEEPS), Jo (good luck in the good old US of A), Audrey (in anticipation of some neat-o floor tiles), Lynne, Lizzie, Nakula, Paul, Timbo, Kurt and all the usual crew, Mum and the family, Jop & Andrea, Jo & Steve & Katie, and Sam, Nick, Ben, Daniel, Gizmo, and Thomas (deceased). Hello to the Psi Corps! Hey, Darren—that death gory enough for ya? Also-rans include all those Down Below at Blackjacks for their cool layouts, Jake Lingwood and Emma Mann—the first two editors on this book. Favorite of the day has to be Jenny Olivier. A big hello to Stephanie Weston, who I last saw age nine. I think we should do lunch more often than once every twenty-five years!! Also, last but not least, a special mention for Simon Lewis and his sexy scaffold, "and about time, too!"

And remember: We Control the Horizontal. We Control the Vertical. They Control the Paychecks. Enjoy! Outtahere—Jimbo.

appendix